Return of the Christmas Spirit

ALSO BY SUSAN BUCHANAN

Return of the Christmas Spirit

Susan Buchanan

COPYRIGHT

DEDICATION

For baby Luke
On your first Christmas
Lots of love, Mummy xxx

ABOUT THE AUTHOR

Susan Buchanan lives in Scotland with her husband, their two young children and a crazy Labrador called Benji. She has been reading since the age of four and had to get an adult library card early as she had read the entire children's section by the age of ten. As a freelance book editor, she has books for breakfast, lunch and dinner and in her personal reading always has several books on the go at any one time.

If she's not reading, editing or writing, she's thinking about it. She loves romantic fiction, psychological thrillers, crime fiction and legal thrillers, but her favourite books feature books themselves.

In her past life she worked in International Sales as she speaks five languages. She has travelled to 51 countries and her travel knowledge tends to pop up in her writing. Collecting books on her travels, even in languages she doesn't speak, became a bit of a hobby.

Susan writes contemporary fiction, partly set in Scotland, usually featuring travel, food or Christmas. When not working, writing, or caring for her two delightful cherubs, Susan loves reading (obviously), the theatre, quiz shows and eating out – not necessarily in that order!

You can connect with Susan via her website (www.susanbuchananauthor.com) or on Facebook (www.facebook.com/susan.buchanan.author) and on Twitter (@susan_buchanan) or Instagram (authorSusanBuchanan).

ACKNOWLEDGEMENTS

Huge thanks to
Wendy Janes for proofreading www.wendyproof.co.uk
Claire at Jaboof Design Studio for my gorgeous cover.
Each one seems to be more beautiful than the last.
claire@jaboofdesignstudio.com
Imogen Howson for eBook formatting www.
imogenhowson.com

Special thanks go to Katy Ferguson, N. E. David, Jim
Watkins and Emma Gray for agreeing to be my beta readers
and for making such a fantastic job of it.

Tracie, Sam and the Chick Lit Goddesses for their input on
too many things to mention, and Tony for doing a lot more
Daddy Day Care than we originally thought would be
necessary, and last but not least my Twitter and Facebook
followers and all the book bloggers who help spread the
word.

CONTENTS

CHAPTER ONE

This is the first time I've been in one of these in I don't know how long, Daniel thought. He grappled for his three-year-old daughter's hand, simultaneously propelling his sons before him, trying to ensure they didn't get caught up in the revolving door. The space he entered wasn't at all what he had expected, and it wasn't simply down to the oversized Scots pine which stood in the centre. His memories of libraries were of musty-smelling, darkened alcoves where sweaty, unwashed students lounged around pretending to work, but actually just procrastinated or flirted with the opposite sex. By contrast, his local library in the small town of Butterburn, where he had lived for the past four years, was a light, airy place, with wooden beams in the ceiling. And rather than the total silence or complete buffoonery which he often encountered at the university library, depending on what time of day he arrived, this establishment seemed to register the low hum of voices. It was, he found, quite calming.

'Look, Daddy, a Christmas tree!' Maya let go of his

hand, rushed forward and started prodding the fake presents which were underneath. 'Does that mean Santa's coming?'

Why, oh why, did businesses have their trees up so early? Daniel wondered. It was always the same; Halloween was barely over and every retail outlet in town started selling Christmas trees. And the adverts on TV – from early November onwards it was impossible to get away from them – and with three kids' attention to deflect from the multitude of toys which were shoved down their throats night after night during the advert breaks, it wasn't always easy. Victoria usually took care of that side of things. She would have prepared a home-cooked meal for them all, fed the kids, and in Maya's case, bathed her, before he arrived home from work. But lately she hadn't been feeling so well. She'd gone to the doctor, but he had been unable to find anything physically wrong with her. It was difficult to put his finger on it; she was more lethargic than anything else, but her sunny disposition had disappeared too. The house, which she kept immaculate, having opted to be a stay-at-home mum, was now constantly in disarray.

'Don't touch, sweetheart. They're not ours.'

'How many more sleeps, Daddy?' His daughter gazed up at him, her eyes full of longing and wonder. *Oh to have her energy and innocence.*

'Still quite a few to go. Right, why don't you show me where Storytime is?'

Dragging him over to the children's section, Maya said, 'Daddy, Daddy, c'mon. It's starting.'

'OK. Dexter, do you want to go and have a look at the books? I take it you're too old for this.'

'Yes, Daddy. I'm eight!'

'Right. Riley, you come with us. Dexter, stay where I can see you.'

'I want to go with Dexter,' moaned his youngest son.

'Roo, you need to come with Daddy. Dex is a big boy.' Riley was only called by his proper name when he misbehaved. From the age of one he'd had a fascination with Winnie the Pooh, and Roo in particular, hence the nickname. The sulky expression on Riley's face told Daniel he wasn't impressed.

Tough. I can't do with him going missing. Daniel had learnt the hard way with Riley. He had a miraculous ability to get lost anywhere he went. He had Daniel and Victoria forever on edge, as often they would turn around and discover that their three children had become two.

Riley shuffled at a snail's pace towards a semicircle of tiny chairs, where a group of around twenty adults were sitting with babies and toddlers of all ages perched on their laps. Some of the bolder ones had ventured further afield and were toddling along, taking books down from the shelves, and in some cases trying to climb into boxes of books. Daniel sighed. This was not his idea of a fun afternoon out. The shrieks and cries of the various children made his temples throb.

A woman, whom he guessed to be in her mid-forties, suddenly appeared and said, 'Good afternoon, everyone.' She then launched into a song, where each parent or grandparent, when their turn came, had to add the name of their child. The children loved it. When the song had ended, Daniel spotted Dexter curled up on one of the leather easy chairs, reading a book which was clearly of interest to him. Daniel then smiled at the sight of five-year-old Riley joining in to 'Incy Wincy Spider', doing all the actions and becoming more animated than any of the toddlers.

By the time the session ended half an hour later, Daniel was startled to realise he hadn't even taken his phone out of his pocket, and had rather enjoyed himself. Dexter was so enthralled in his book he didn't even notice his father towering over him, until he asked him what he was reading. *The Bad Beginning*, part of Lemony Snicket's 'A Series of Unfortunate Events'. Made sense – Dexter was currently into anything where the hero was naughty or where gruesome events befell the characters, but he liked his books to be funny too.

Maya wanted to take out some books, so Daniel stood patiently whilst she handed him *Peppa Pig: Peppa Goes Swimming*, *Hairy Maclary's Bone* and *Dear Zoo*. He took the books, and those the boys had chosen, to the desk which said Enquiries. The librarian who had chaired the Storytime session glanced up at him, took in the books Daniel was holding and said to Maya, 'Ah, fine choices. Are these for you, young lady?'

Maya, apparently overcome with shyness, hid behind her father at first, but then popped her head out and nodded.

'Have you read *Rumpus at the Vet*? It's one of my favourite Hairy Maclary books,' the librarian said, as she stamped the dates on the books.

'No. What's it about?'

Star, what an unusual name, thought Daniel, as he read it off the badge on her blouse. Parents must have been hippies.

Seeing him looking, Star finished the explanation she was giving Maya and then said, 'My father was an astrologer. It was that or Cassiopeia.'

'Sorry. I didn't mean to stare. It's just so unusual.'

'Yes, although there were seven hundred and forty of us in the UK at last count.'

'Really?' *How do they even know such a thing?*

'Oh yes, I'm not as unique as you might think,' She beamed at him.

'Right,' said Daniel awkwardly.

'Why don't I give you a call when the vet book comes in, Mr Fairchild?'

'That would be great, thanks,' Daniel said, pleasantly surprised at such a personal service, and delighted as it had caused a huge smile to break across Maya's face.

Maya waved goodbye to Star, then took hold of her father's hand. 'She was a nice lady, Daddy, and she had a pretty name.'

'Yes.' Daniel's thoughts were elsewhere. There was something about Star which unsettled him. Maybe she reminded him of someone.

'Who wants pizza for tea?'

'Me, me, me!' came three voices in unison.

Now he just had to make it.

As Star watched the family walk away, she smiled to herself. That Maya was a cutie and she had her father wrapped around her finger. He had looked tired, frazzled even, but she'd soon sort that. She was enjoying her new placement. The other librarians were kind overall, although some were a little gossipy, and it had been a blow that she hadn't been able to spend time with Anne-Marie whose maternity leave she was covering, but Anne-Marie didn't need her help. She had a loving family around her and a wonderful husband who would prove a doting dad when the baby arrived in a few months. Star had to concentrate on those who needed her. Daniel was the first of her four charges this year.

'Hey, Star, that's not fair. You've just arrived and you've immediately zoned in on the "hottie"!' exclaimed Bridget, one of the other librarians. 'So, spill the beans,' she said, as she gathered a pile of books waiting to go back on the shelves and bundled them into the cart.

When Star told her about the books the children had taken out, Jessica, Bridget's sidekick, broke in, 'We don't want to know about the books. Is he divorced or separated at least?'

'I didn't ask him about his personal life.'

'Shame. Next time he's in, I'm asking him if his wife wouldn't like to bring the kids sometime.' Bridget was evidently pleased with her cunning plan on how to find out if he was married or not. 'We may be married, but there's no harm in window-shopping and that man was one fine-looking piece of eye candy.'

'He certainly was. Good idea,' Jessica said, putting her arm around her colleague in congratulation.

Seeing another customer approach the desk, Star made her excuses and escaped.

'Sorry,' a young girl's voice said as Star felt the wind being knocked out of her, the pile of books she was carrying falling from her hands and toppling to the ground. 'Are you OK?'

'I'm fine,' Star reassured her, righting her glasses, which had gone askew. As the girl, who had to be in her mid-teens, scrabbled around picking up all the books off the floor, Star appraised her.

'I'm so clumsy.'

'No harm done. Studying?' she asked, indicating the girl's backpack.

'Yes. Mocks coming up.'

'Thought so. You were here the other day, weren't you?'

'I come here most days after school. It's a good place to study and Mum doesn't like me being in the house alone before she gets in from work.'

'You're right. It is a good place to study. I only started this week, but it's quite relaxed here. So, what are you studying?'

'English, history, physics, maths and music,' the girl rhymed off.

'Quite a busy timetable you have. Well, I'd better not hold you up any further. I'm Star. Let me know if you need anything.'

The girl nodded, then seemed to realise Star was waiting for something. 'Arianna.' She hesitated momentarily then added, 'Gray.'

'Arianna. That's a beautiful name, unusual. From the Greek, meaning very holy or chaste. But I expect you knew that. Linked to Ariadne, the daughter of King Minos, who helped Theseus escape from the labyrinth after he killed the Minotaur. Sorry, I'm a big fan of mythology. Did you ever study classical mythology?'

'Yes, I know the story of King Minos, but I'd never thought about the connection between Ariadne and Arianna. I suppose they are pretty similar. That's kinda cool.'

'Very cool,' Star agreed. 'Well, Arianna, it was lovely to talk to you and like I said, I'm here to help.'

'OK. Thanks.'

As Star replaced the books on the shelves, she watched the retreating back of the teenager with the long, curly black hair, smiled and gave herself a little tick. Two down, two to go.

CHAPTER TWO

The next day the library was busy from the moment it opened.

'Star, could you go upstairs and check on the PC users, please?' Jessica asked. 'I think a couple may have run over their time slots and there are people waiting. I'm a little busy right now, or I'd do it myself.'

'No problem.' Star was keen to become involved in all aspects of the library and so far that day had ordered books, repaired some of the children's books which had been returned in a less than pristine condition, contacted the printers for more leaflets for the Christmas book sessions which had started a couple of days before, as well as helping out on the Enquiries desk. The lofty heights, literally, of the first-floor Reference and Computing sections had remained out of her reach until now. She picked up the schedule which showed the time slots and names against each PC and headed upstairs.

'Excuse me, Mr Donnelly, I think you may have run over your time. Have you finished what you're doing?' Star asked.

With a weak smile, which didn't quite reach his striking blue eyes, the man said, 'Not quite, but I'll be back tomorrow, anyway.'

Star thanked him and scanned her list to see which other users were over their allotted time.

Evan saved his file, emailed it to himself and logged out of his account. Running a hand through his wavy blond hair, which was turning greyer every day, he sighed and prayed one of the many tailored emails he had sent off that day would amount to something. Sitting here today had reminded him of the dozens of CVs he'd sent off over the past two years, for much more junior positions than the managerial ones he had held in the past. Most companies didn't even deign to reply, never mind offer him an interview. After he lost his job as R&D director at an engineering firm, and with no vacancies forthcoming in his field, retraining in IT security had sounded an excellent idea. His salary hadn't been astronomical, but he had been comfortable. Well, he certainly wasn't comfortable now. He'd sent out countless applications for IT positions, buoyed by the many times the media had said there was a skills shortage in that area, but the reality was employers wanted someone with the exact skill set they required, not someone, especially at his age, just starting out. And Evan simply couldn't get an interview.

He felt humiliated that he had had to resort to bar work to survive. Oh, bar work was fine for a young person at university as a part-time job, but it wasn't going to pay the bills for a forty-seven-year-old man with two kids, a wife and the sort of lifestyle they had grown accustomed to. Had it not been for the strain and worry of how to pay his debts, he might have enjoyed working at The Dog and Ferret, even though his boss was a git, but since washing glasses, pouring pints and cleaning sticky tables wasn't seen as a skilled job, the pay was hardly worth getting out of bed for.

As he slipped on his jacket and packed away his things, Evan asked himself when he had last had a night out, when he had last done something for himself, something which didn't involve working to try to get him and his family out of debt. Four months? Six? It wasn't quite a year, but it was a long time ago.

Evan descended the staircase in the open-plan library and saw that a group of around fifteen people had congregated in one corner. Curious, he sidled over to see what was so interesting. Copies of John Grisham's *Skipping Christmas* lay on a table. He waited expectantly.

'Good evening, everyone.'

Evan whirled around. There was the woman who had told him he had overrun his computer time.

'Thanks for coming. Can I ask how many of you have already read *Skipping Christmas*?'

A show of hands indicated that around half had. Skipping Christmas sounded like a great idea to Evan right now. He had no idea how he was going to pay for it all. They could no longer indulge in the type of Christmases they had been lucky enough to have to date. Already he and his wife, Louise, had been curbing their excesses, trying to stretch their pay packets a bit further. Unfortunately, it wasn't enough. The debts weren't coming down. Instead, on a daily basis, he felt as if matters were spiralling increasingly out of control, and the lack of a decent job did little to assuage his anguish.

On a whim, Evan decided to sit in on the book session. It wasn't as if he had money to go and do anything else, anyway. He assumed it was free, and hoped he was right. As he listened to those who had read the book discuss it, he found that he quite fancied it, although it wasn't his usual read. He preferred psychological thrillers or detective stories, but it sounded that tiny bit different, and he was feeling a bit 'bah, humbug' himself. The librarian was an engaging sort and kept the conversation flowing between the various participants, not allowing any one person to monopolise the discussion.

Forty-five minutes later, Evan felt a little lighter. OK, it was fiction, but even so, he could take some comfort in the fact others had problems, lives that weren't perfect and that they had to cope with the holiday season too.

As he rose to leave, a hand rested gently on his shoulder. 'You didn't take a copy. You haven't read it yet, am I right?' the librarian he'd met earlier asked him, a smile on her lips.

'No-o-o, I haven't,' Evan stammered, taken aback anyone had singled him out to speak to. These days he felt invisible. He hadn't thought that, back when he had a place, a proper place in society, when he knew what his purpose was in life. He had been good at his job, but it just went to show, there was no job security any more. No matter how hard he had worked, in both his engineering roles and in his attempt at a new career in IT security, it hadn't made any difference. He was a failure. And he didn't see how that was going to change any time soon, if the lack of replies to the CVs he had sent out was anything to go by. He took the book from the woman's outstretched hand, thanked her and went to the desk to check it out, feeling cheered for the first time in months. There's still goodness in the world, after all, he thought.

This sucks, thought Arianna for the umpteenth time, as she twirled her hair around her index finger. She jabbed her notebook repeatedly with her pen, as if by doing so, divine inspiration might strike. *God, I hate physics. Why did I agree to take this subject?* She knew why; her science teacher had pressured her into it, telling her she had done well enough on her GCSEs that she should take at least one science subject and possibly two. Arianna had baulked at that suggestion, but relented on the idea of taking one science subject and been pushed towards physics, apparently the more cerebral of the sciences. 'Says who?' she wondered, as she scowled at her blank page again. She hadn't a clue. If things continued like this she'd fail all her mocks, not only physics, as she had no time to dedicate to anything else, because she spent so much time studying physics. Maybe she should give it up as a lost cause and concentrate on her other subjects, but she so hated to fail. She was in real danger of screwing up maths too, although fortunately she was a natural at history, music and English, so didn't think she would flunk those. However, she did worry that she might not get the grades she wanted, what with studying for the dreaded physics and maths. Was she ever going to use them in the real world?

She wished her dad were here. He'd know what to do, or rather 'old' dad would. Dad before he abandoned her, because let's be honest, that's what he'd done, discarded her like a used sweet wrapper, when he'd separated from her mum. Now she was lucky if she got a phone call from him once a week. Yeah, yeah, she knew he lived in Dubai and calls were expensive, but no one asked him to move to

Dubai, did they? Arianna felt herself tense. Every time she thought of her dad and his new life she felt sick. She would never have left her mum, but it would have been nice to have been asked if she wanted to go and live with him, or even come for a holiday. But zilch, diddly squat. Now it seemed he didn't care about her. She had no dad to speak of, no money, no friends and no social life.

Oh, her friends stuck around for a while after her dad left. At least until her mum said sorry she couldn't have fifteen pounds to go to the cinema; no, she couldn't have a new top for the party on Saturday; and no, she didn't have the money to pay for her badminton club now either. As her mum's finances dwindled, so did Arianna's group of friends. They got bored of her saying she couldn't do anything or go anywhere because she had no money. Oh, initially they tried to shrug it off. 'No biggie,' 'Next time,' they said. 'Oh, it will probably be crap, anyway.' 'You aren't missing much.' But over time, and one by one, they had fallen away. She was better off without them. They weren't real friends. They hadn't been there when she needed them. She'd show them. She'd get the best grades in the year and then she'd have the pick of all the universities when she left school. Who cared if Darren Neilson said Aimee's highlights made her look fit, or if Garry Lappin thought Cleo was a babe.

If only she wasn't so damned tired. Between studying and doing as much of the housework as possible to ease the burden on her mum, who was working three jobs: taxi controller, assistant in a Chinese takeaway and cleaner in a school, she was exhausted. But her mum wanted them to move to a better area, escape the run-down council estate they were living in, where they'd been forced to move to, following her parents' split. Surely she shouldn't be this tired at sixteen, exams or no exams? She'd even gone to the doctor. He'd told her she needed more physical exercise. Well, she had been getting plenty of exercise when she'd been playing badminton four times a week, but between exams, no money to pay for sessions and helping her mum, she was only exercising at school P.E. times. And she was considering being a P.E. teacher. Yeah, that was a laugh. If she could just concentrate. She spent so much time in the library but wasn't sure how much she actually achieved, despite her efforts. She scrambled around searching for the answers in her head, which felt kind of woolly these days.

Sitting upright, Arianna decided she could do with a break. She stretched out her long legs beneath the desk and her arms overhead, and oblivious to who saw her, she tried to release some of the tension from her body, before standing up and going into the stacks to look for the maths reference book she knew she needed for later. The Internet was great, but sometimes it had too much choice and you spent more time trawling through the endless possibilities, when in fact all the information you required was within the pages of a book.

Arianna couldn't find the reference guide she'd been looking for, so decided to see if someone had moved it by mistake onto one of the shelves around it. Nope. Nothing. As she backed up, ready to return to her table, she didn't notice the person behind her do the same thing from the opposite direction. 'Ow!' yelped a voice at the same time as Arianna's own. Turning round, she came face to face with the school tie of St Joseph's. Looking up, she met the first apologetic, then smiling brown eyes of a boy who had to be around her age.

'Sorry. I wasn't watching where I was going.'

'Me neither.' Arianna found her heart was pounding, and for once was glad of her clumsiness.

After a momentary silence, he said, 'You studying too?'

Arianna looked at the books in the boy's hands. Four maths books. One of them was the book she had been hoping to take out. *So that's where it went.*

Her mouth suddenly dry, Arianna gulped, trying to find some saliva so she could speak. *C'mon*, she willed herself, *say something scintillating*. She nodded.

'What you studying?'

Finding her voice this time, Arianna replied, 'Physics and maths.' She indicated one of the books he was holding. 'I don't suppose I could borrow that after you're done with it? That's the book I was just looking for.'

'Here, have it.' He held out the book to her.

'Are you sure?' she asked, delighted at his generosity.

'Positive.' He grinned. 'I have these three for bedtime reading already.'

Reddening at his innocent mention of bedtime, Arianna mumbled her thanks and said she ought to get back to studying.

'See you around.' He smiled at her.

'Yeah, see you.'

Arianna sat back down at her desk, suddenly aware she didn't know his name. After reading through the first pages of the book he'd lent her, and taking none of it in, she gave up and daydreamed instead about how she could have prolonged the conversation with him. What did he look like? A Michael, a Finn, a James? Nope. She wondered if he studied here. She hadn't seen him before. Giving this evening's study session up for lost, Arianna packed away her things and booked out the maths guide. As she walked the mile back to her house, she felt somehow the world had become a little bit brighter.

'Is that you, hon?' Louise's voice came from the kitchen as Evan locked the front door behind him.

'Yep.'

Gone were the days when he'd come home shouting, 'Honey, I'm home!' like a character from an American sitcom. He simply couldn't muster up the enthusiasm. But tonight he felt lighter than he had in ages. Placing *Skipping Christmas* on the hall table where he always left his keys, his loose change and his wallet, Evan pushed open the kitchen door and went in to greet his wife. She was wearing her pale blue care assistant uniform, with her hair pulled back in a hastily arranged ponytail. How he hated that uniform. It was bland and highlighted to him how far they had fallen. When times had been good, Louise hadn't needed to work. He reminded himself he was lucky that he had a gem of a wife. She had stuck by him when times had got tough, really tough. She had been the one to suggest she get a job, although in the beginning they had expected it would be a part-time one. Evan thought she was a saint, for everything she did, and for everything she had put up with. She'd taken their fall from grace in her stride: the neighbours gossiping, having to remove their son, Ryan, from the private school they had so carefully chosen for him. She hadn't been fazed by any of it. She was the one constant in his life. He had to remember that. Many wives would have left their husbands at such a massive change in circumstances. The shock to the system would have been too great.

As he kissed Louise hello and listened to the many

instructions she gave him: what the kids were to have for dinner, that he needed to fix the leaky tap in the bathroom, how he had to choose a new gas and electricity tariff as theirs was coming to an end, that the bins hadn't been emptied yet, and that his mum had called and asked for him to call her back, Evan knew he was lucky. If he could only get a job, a real job, with decent pay and regular hours, perhaps everything would work out.

CHAPTER THREE

Star was arranging the storyboard from St Luke's Primary outlining the Christmas traditions in the Czech Republic when a voice broke into her train of thought.

'So what did you do before you came here?' Jessica asked her.

'I worked in a bakery café in Winstanton.' Of course, back then her name hadn't been Star.

'Winstanton. Is that in the Lake District?' Bridget asked.

'No, it's in Scotland, near Loch Lomond,' Star told her, as she sorted a pile of books into alphabetical order.

'Lovely part of the world. How long were you there?'

'Not long,' Star said, hiding a smile at Jessica's nosiness.

Jessica and Bridget exchanged a look – a look which said, 'She's not giving much away, is she?' Thwarted for juicy details for now, they changed the subject and Star got back to arranging the Christmas tradition board. What an inspired idea. She knew the majority, if not all, of the Christmas traditions throughout the world, but she imagined most people wouldn't. She was, of course, in the business. The library post was merely a secondary job for her. However, she derived great pleasure reading about the traditions and was heartened to see the schoolchildren had learnt the different customs in other parts of the world.

She'd always thought that those in certain parts of Europe, including the Czech Republic and the Netherlands had a good deal, as they really got to celebrate Christmas twice, once with *Mikulas* on 5 December, or *Sinterklaas* on 6 December, and again with Santa Claus on the twenty-fourth or twenty-fifth. She had been performing her Christmas role for a very long time, and had seen many traditions change over her tenure. She read on, '*Children recite a poem or song, and St Nicholas gives them a little basket of presents, often filled with chocolate. He is accompanied by devils and angels. Merry Christmas in Czech is* Prejeme Vam Vesele Vanoce.' There was more detail, which Star read, and she wondered which country would be represented the next day.

The Christmas storyboards had been the brainchild of the assistant head at St Jude's Primary in Hawksmeade, and all of the surrounding primary schools had been allocated a country to research and choose which pieces of Christmas trivia would appear on their storyboard. On 22 December, there was to be a big event at the library with canapés and drinks, and all the storyboards would be seen together for the first time, kind of like a Christmas art exhibition. Star thought it was wonderful and had told her manager from the outset that she was keen to be involved.

Moving on to her next task, she couldn't help thinking there seemed to be an interminable number of books to put away this morning, as she sorted yet another hundred or so ready to go back on the shelves. And she still had some repairs to do too. She imagined children's books always needed taping back together. Glancing at the children's section she could see quite a few were beyond tatty. She'd work on those shortly, but first she had to pay a visit to the ladies'.

Star opened the door to the staff toilets and stopped dead. A quiet sobbing, indistinct but discernible, could be heard coming from one of the cubicles. She didn't want to intrude, but she also didn't want to abandon whoever was in such terrible distress. She waited. Whoever was inside had obviously heard her come in, as the crying had stopped, to be replaced by a quiet sniffing. Soon afterwards the cubicle door opened and Star came face to face with her startled boss, Patricia Thackeray.

'Oh, I thought you'd gone,' she said.

'No. I wanted to see if you were all right.'

'Yes, I'm fine.' Patricia turned on the taps and splashed water on her face, causing her mascara to run in rivulets down her cheeks. 'Dammit!' she shouted at the mirror, then burst into tears again. Noisy, hiccupping sobs this time.

Star passed her a packet of make-up removal wipes from her bag.

Patricia shot her a grateful glance. 'Thanks,' she managed before she was wracked again by more sobs. 'I don't usually do this.' She tried to compose herself, but then burst out, half laughing, 'But then my husband of twenty-three years doesn't usually leave me.' And with that she was off again, crying uncontrollably.

Star laid her hand on Patricia's arm in a comforting gesture. She didn't say anything, but waited to see if she wanted to confide further in her. She wasn't going to push.

Once Patricia stopped crying, she blew her nose, then turned to Star and apologised again.

'There's nothing to be sorry for.'

'It's all such a mess,' she began. 'And it's so clichéd it's a joke.' The expression on her face revealed it was anything but. 'His secretary, for goodness' sake! He could at least have shown a bit of originality.'

Star made the right noises in the right places, giving Patricia the confidence to continue.

'Oh, and it would have to happen now when Anne-Marie's away.'

'Anne-Marie?'

'Anne-Marie whose maternity leave you're covering. She's my best friend. But she's seven and a half months pregnant. I can't bother her with this...' She searched for the right word. '...fiasco.'

Star could understand why she was reluctant to burden her friend, but equally thought Anne-Marie might be more resilient than Patricia gave her credit for. 'Isn't there anyone else you can talk to about it?'

'No, not really.' Patricia wiped the streaks of mascara from her cheeks. 'I have a sister who lives in Italy now, but it's not the kind of thing I want to discuss over the phone.'

Star nodded her understanding.

Patricia took a brush from her bag and dragged it through her soft blonde bob whilst she composed herself. Freshened up, she took a deep breath, squared her shoulders and said, 'Thank you. Sorry to offload my problems on you – so unprofessional of me. It's only just happened, you see.'

'Don't mention it. If you ever want to talk, I'm here,' Star said as she held the door open for her.

As they walked back towards the stacks, Star hoped Patricia had taken her comment on board. Her boss was in need of a friend.

. . .

'So where are you staying?' Jessica asked Star. 'Have you bought somewhere or are you renting?'

'Well, it's only a maternity contract so I'm renting for now.' She never gave away any more than she had to, and she did derive a little naughty pleasure in being so sparing with the details, when Jessica and Bridget were so clearly dying to know all about her.

'And does your husband like it here?' fished Bridget.

'Oh, I'm not married.'

'I haven't put my foot in it, have I?' said Bridget. 'He hasn't…' she inclined her head, then said '…passed?'

'No, I'm not widowed. I never married.'

Bridget and Jessica exchanged a knowing look. 'Do you have a partner?' Jessica was intent on ascertaining her romantic status.

'Not at the moment.' Star remained vague. 'Oh, are you here to collect your book, Maya?' she asked, as the little girl reached the Enquiries desk.

Foiled again, Jessica returned to the computer system to update some records and Bridget trundled off with a trolley of books. Star hid a grin and then smiled when Maya turned to her father and said, 'Daddy, the lady 'membered my name!'

'Yes, I wonder why that is,' Daniel said, his eyes raised heavenward.

'Here you go, Maya. *Rumpus at the Vet*.' Star handed the book to her. 'Are you coming to the storytelling session? It's just about to start.'

Maya looked up at her father, who checked his watch, seemed to try to do some calculation in his head, then sighing said, 'OK, but we have to head off straight after.'

'Hurrah!' Maya's enthusiasm was infectious.

Maya sat in the Storytime circle with the other children, then Riley slunk over too, and even Dexter let himself be led in that general direction.

Dr Seuss' *The Grinch Who Stole Christmas* more than occupied everyone's attention, with Star giving each of the characters different voices and encouraging the children to participate.

Daniel stretched out his long legs as much as he could on the child seat and scrolled through his messages. He'd had the foresight to turn off the sound on his phone. Being silent in a library must have been instilled in me when I was little, he thought. He toyed with just relaxing for a few minutes or even listening to the story, one he had loved as a boy, but he had too much to do.

Work alone was a nightmare at the moment, what with shouldering the workload of three people. Joe was on long-term sick leave, and Archie had upped and left a month ago – gone to a competitor, taking his client list with him if Daniel's irate boss was to be believed. Neither had been replaced, not even temporarily, and as far as Daniel knew the company wasn't actively recruiting for replacements. How his boss, Craig, expected him to deal with his own sales territory and theirs he didn't know. He really needed to have a chat with him, but wasn't sure how to approach it, as everyone feared for their jobs these days. Revenue wasn't what it once was, and margins were being squeezed tighter than ever. Bonuses had been cut for the past three years in a row. That was all very well for top management, but the bods on the street relied on those bonuses, as their basic salaries weren't high. It had always been an unwritten rule that field sales managers made most of their wages from bonus or commission rather than from their basic wage, but now that trend was on the slide.

The whisky industry was a cut-throat one and keeping your customers solely on loyalty was becoming more and more difficult. With all this in mind, Daniel did his best to keep on top of his workload. There would always be a competitor nipping at his heels trying to drive him out of a contract, and with his company's reduced manpower, ensuring he was able to provide the best service to his customers wasn't proving easy.

At Maya's voice, Daniel glanced up. She was reciting some of the lines from the book Star had been reading to the children. It looked like she was trying to get some of the older ones to take the parts of some of the characters. How he wished he had more time to get involved.

His mind drifted away from the storytelling session as he pondered how thin he was stretched. Work was bad enough, but Victoria wasn't fit to do half the chores she normally did for the family. At first he'd thought she had a bad case of flu, the real thing, not just a stinking cold. She was so sluggish and could hardly get out of bed. Her energy had gone and nothing held any interest for her. Her incredible green eyes had dulled, her normally lustrous copper curls lank. His beautiful wife evidently wasn't herself, but it was all he could do to get through each day at the moment. Between work and caring for the children as much as he could, in the light of Victoria's illness, he had little time left over to wonder what was afflicting his wife. He'd suggested she go back to the doctor, but she'd refused, saying he'd said she was fine, simply a little run-down. She just needed a bit of a break, a rest. Well, that was all very well, but how? They had no family close by. Daniel's parents had retired to Northern Ireland, Victoria's father was dead and her mother was in a nursing home. Both were only children, so they couldn't even farm the children out to aunts and uncles.

Daniel's thoughts strayed to the housework which awaited him on his return home. He wondered if Victoria had managed to take the washing out of the machine and put it in the tumble dryer. He was running out of clothes for them to wear. This morning he'd chosen clothes that despite not having been ironed, looked as if they had. That was another thing he had to do – look for a company to send the ironing out to. He could iron, of course he could, but he didn't have time. And some of the kids' clothes did need ironing and all of his work shirts and trousers did too. Currently he ironed a shirt the day he wore it. The ironing baskets were overflowing, as were the dirty laundry baskets. It amazed him how much washing three children could produce. OK, he could have understood if they had a baby or even a toddler, but Maya, the youngest, was three. He found himself empathising with Victoria. Raising kids, being a stay-at-home mum, was hard work. Much harder than he had ever appreciated.

He looked at his watch again. Quarter past eleven. If they left at half past, they should be able to make it to Dexter's football match with just enough time for him to change into his strip. Ideally Victoria could have taken either Dexter or kept the two youngest, but since she wasn't up to it, he'd had to bring the three of them to the library, which now meant they all had to sit through the football match. That would be a nightmare with Maya, thought Daniel. Even Riley would lose interest after fifteen minutes or so. At least they would have books to read. He wondered if he'd packed their Nintendo DS.

The session drew to a close and Daniel took his

daughter's hand when she held it out to him, and pulled her up. He ruffled her hair and she complained, 'Dad. You'll make my ribbon come out again!'

He bloomin' hoped not. It had taken him forever to put it in this morning. He hadn't had much call to plait hair until now. Maya held out her arms to her father, beseeching him to lift her up, which he duly did. She snuggled into his neck.

'Are you tired, sweetheart?'

'Mmm,' Maya said, already half-asleep on the crook of his neck.

Well, she had been up early, half past five or thereabouts. There was no such thing as a lie-in for him these days. He barely got any sleep. Sometimes he felt at least a decade older than his thirty-two years. Despite his resolve to leave as soon as Storytime was over, Daniel stopped by the public notice board to see if there were any ironing company adverts listed. There weren't. Oh well…

Just then, Star pinned up a notice.

Cleaner – Honest and reliable with great references

£7 per hour. Butterburn, Hawksmeade and surrounding areas.

Own Transport

The phone number followed. Taking out his mobile, Daniel saved the number to memory, rounded up his sons, whilst still cradling Maya in one arm, and headed out to his car. Maybe the cleaner would iron too. As he recalled the state of his living room and kitchen this morning before they left, he thought perhaps the cleaner would be the answer to at least some of his problems.

CHAPTER FOUR

'Did you not see her in here the other day?' Bridget whispered to Jessica. 'Looked to me like she'd been crying.'

'Do you think we should say something?' Jessica asked.

'No. What would we say? "How are you doing, Patricia? Your husband's left you and not even for a better-looking model, but just his plain, fifty-something secretary." I'm not even sure she's younger. What is Patricia, fifty-four? I know she takes care of herself, so she could be older.'

'No, Patricia's fifty-two. She's exactly a year older than me. We have the same birthday. I always thought that Ian was a bit of a charmer. Not a bad-looking man, at all.'

'I didn't realise you shared a birthday. I guess I'm the baby then, at fifty-one! No, Ian's not my type. I'd rather have my Davie any day,' Bridget said. 'Ian's too smarmy. He has a bit of the car salesman about him.'

'I know just what you mean. He's better-looking than my husband, if we're honest, but at least William isn't likely to run off with his secretary.'

Star, who was standing on the other side of the stacks to them, and who was hidden by the rows of books, understood why Patricia had no one here she could confide in, except maybe her. Jessica and Bridget were nice enough in their own ways, but keeping confidences wasn't one of their traits. Star glanced over to the Enquiries desk where Patricia was going through the motions, pasting on a bright smile for the public. She still wore her clothes with elegance and her make-up was flawless, yet no amount of cosmetics could cover the bags under her eyes, which hinted at sleepless nights. Star decided to see if she could cheer her up. The library's café, Scrolls, a project which had taken more than a year to complete, had opened the day before.

'Do you fancy a coffee at lunchtime?' Star asked Patricia when they met at the Enquiries desk a few minutes later. 'We really ought to try out Scrolls. It's almost our duty.'

Initially reticent, Patricia was won over by Star's warm smile. 'I'd like that.'

'Excellent.' And with that, Star went off to tackle Bridget about the whereabouts of the materials for the children's Christmas card-making event that afternoon.

'This coffee's lovely,' said Patricia.

'It is pretty good, isn't it?' Star agreed. She waited a few moments, then when Patricia wasn't forthcoming, asked her how she was.

'OK, I suppose.' She stopped. 'Well, no, not great, if truth be told. I'm not sleeping and I'm exhausted. I need to get some sleep soon. I just feel so stupid. How could I not have known? I genuinely didn't, you know. They always say the wife's the last to know, but I always thought that was moronic. I naively assumed they must be turning a blind eye. But when it happened to me, I understood how it was possible. He must have been so careful. But then, I trusted Ian. I had no reason not to.'

Star nodded and let her continue.

'And I don't know how we're going to tell the kids. I know they're in their twenties, but they'll be so shocked. I'm not looking forward to it. Megan's a total daddy's girl. She'll be devastated.'

Star murmured reassurance and Patricia went on, 'As for Graeme, my son, he idolises my husband. The thought that his father might screw up, or screw around–' she laughed bitterly '–will deeply affect him. And the timing couldn't be worse, with Christmas coming up. Thanks, Ian. Merry blooming Christmas. And I don't even get to be pleased in some small way, that I don't have his annoying habits to live with any more. He's tidier than me, can cook well and is a perfect gent – apart from the small matter of having a bit on the side. Although, now she's not the bit on the side, is she? She's the main event. I'm just the cast-off.'

All the oomph suddenly appeared to go out of her and she sank back in the leather armchair. 'Oh God, what am I going to do?' She leant forward, her head in her hands. Her voice low, not wishing to attract attention to herself, she said, 'I don't know how to be single. It's been such a long time. I don't mean from a "having another partner" point of view,' she clarified, 'but I've been part of a pair for so long, there are things I don't know how to do on my own.'

'What sort of things?' Star asked.

'Well, apart from macho things like mending electrical appliances which blow up, fixing leaks and changing tyres, other stuff like juggling finances, finding the best deal on car insurance, as well as going to dinner parties and other events. We had quite an active social life, a wide circle of friends.'

'You'll manage. It won't always be easy, but life has ways of helping you down the right path. You've heard the saying "one door closes, another one opens"?'

'Yes. It just seems as if they're all closing in my face right now,' she said sadly.

'It won't always be that way,' Star said. 'Some good will come of this, I promise you. It's hard to believe or understand right now, but it will.'

'I hope you're right.' Patricia drained her coffee. 'You ready?' she said, swinging her bag onto her shoulder. 'Time to head back.'

'Look, I know she's working today, I need to see her,' came a shrill voice as Star opened the main door to the library.

'Megan?' said Patricia from behind her, surprise at seeing her daughter evident in her tone.

She hurried over and took her to one side. 'What are you doing here? Is everything OK? Who's watching the kids?'

'The kids are fine. Mum, I know about you and Dad. I drove all the way here as soon as I heard.'

Patricia knew Megan hated driving and would only have made the five-hundred-mile round trip from Cardiff if she thought she had to. Her shoulders slumped and she visibly sagged.

'Who told you?'

'Dad, of course. How could you, Mum? How could you throw him out?'

'Wha-a-a-t?' Patricia choked out. She was hurt, but not surprised, that her daughter had taken her father's side.

'Dad said you threw him out, that you were really unreasonable and he had no choice but to go and stay with friends.'

Flabbergasted and furious in equal measure, Patricia pulled herself up to her full height again and said, 'That's not what happened.'

'What were you thinking?'

Seeing the library was busy, Patricia said, 'I can't talk about this right now. We have customers, but wait until we get home tonight and we can have a chat.'

'I've got to be back in Cardiff for a meeting tomorrow morning. I can't.'

'Well, a phone call will have to do then, or you can wait until it's quieter here.'

Chewing her lip as if it helped her decision-making process, Megan said, 'I'll wait.'

'But, Dad, everyone has a PlayStation 4 these days. How can I play if I don't have one?' Ryan said, his tone exasperated.

Evan looked at his son in dismay. He had always wanted to give his kids everything. That was the crux of the problem. They weren't adapting to this more meagre lifestyle. He wasn't even sure they were able to comprehend the severity of their situation. Evan felt certain that at thirteen, had his father told him they didn't have the money for something, he would have taken that at face value, and not expected the same number of treats he had been lucky enough to enjoy in the past. Although it had now been two years since Evan lost his job as R&D

Director, the news that they didn't have the same amount of money seemed not to apply to Ryan, or Georgia. Only the other day she had asked for a pony. A pony, for heaven's sake! He wondered what his mother would have said to him, if he'd asked for such a thing at the age of ten. No doubt she'd have laughed in his face at the absurd request.

Georgia had asked last year, and to get her off his back, and because he genuinely thought his work situation would have sorted itself out, he'd foolishly said she could have one next year. Next year was now. Why couldn't she have wanted a pony when he was making good money? He could have easily afforded it then. He had been living the dream. Now he was living the nightmare. Georgia still wasn't speaking to him.

'Ryan, we've already had this conversation. You said you wanted a bike for Christmas and that's what we've bought you.' Evan didn't add that he'd had to get into more debt to buy it. He'd figure out later how to pay it back. When he'd bought it, he'd done so feeling sad and aggrieved that the kids had gone without so much this year, but when his son behaved like a spoilt brat, it made him think twice. But then whose fault was it if Ryan was spoilt?

'Ryan.' Evan fought to keep his voice calm. 'We can't afford to get you a new PlayStation. Look, I've got to get to work. If I don't go now, I'll miss the bus.'

Ryan stormed off. Sighing, Evan located his jacket and house keys and shouted upstairs, 'I'm away, Lou. I'm late. See you tonight.'

'Bye,' shouted Louise as Evan closed the front door behind him and raced to the bus stop.

. . .

I hate buses, thought Evan, as he waited on the number 23 to Hawksmeade. Prior to his fall from grace, he hadn't been on a bus in more than a decade, unless you counted a sightseeing tour bus in New York. Now, with his Mercedes long gone and Lou needing the eight-year-old Renault Clio to get around for work, the bus was his only way of getting to work. Evan laughed out loud. He wouldn't be working in a bar if he still had his Merc. Although he knew it had been an extravagance, and that it was a material possession, and let's face it, an indication of wealth which he no longer had, he couldn't help missing it. It had been so damned comfortable and it was his, his haven, his place of respite. He'd actually enjoyed the drive to work in the morning. His transport finally arrived, and climbing aboard, Evan gave a rueful smile yet again at just how far he had fallen.

'You're late, mate,' said the bar manager when he arrived.

'Sorry, I know. It's those roadworks on Station Road – they're a killer. The bus should have got in at five to five.'

'Well, I'll have to dock you quarter of an hour, I'm afraid,' said his boss, not looking remotely sorry about it. 'Now, those tables need clearing, and once you've done that, there's a couple of bin bags of Christmas decorations in the cellar. Bring them up and help Sian put them up when you get a minute later.'

Ho, ho, ho, thought Evan. How hypocritical. His boss made Scrooge seem generous.

Looking around the already crowded pub, Evan wondered when he would get a chance to put up the decorations. The pints were cheap here, so it was always busy. Realising he was in for a busy stint tonight, he sighed and started clearing the glasses and empty crisp packets off the table in front of him.

'So, what's going on?' Megan tried again once the library had cleared to a more manageable level almost an hour later. 'Did you throw Dad out?'

'No.'

'No?' Megan's eyebrows knitted together in confusion.

'He left.'

'Why did he leave? What did you say to him?' Megan's tone was accusatory.

'I didn't say much, at all, as it happens.'

'What d'you mean?'

'Well, it was your father who had quite the revelation to make. What exactly did he tell you?'

As Patricia listened to the lies Ian had told Megan she went from feeling deflated to apoplectic.

'I think it'd be fair to say your dad hasn't told us the same story. Perhaps you should ask him what he told me?'

'Mum, enough of this messing around. I've already waited for an hour to talk to you. What is going on?'

Hating Ian for ensuring she was the bearer of bad news and not him, how typical, she decided to tell her daughter and to hell with him. Maybe his little princess wouldn't look so favourably on her father when she found out what he had been up to.

'I'm sorry, darling, I really am, but your father told me he's been seeing someone else and he's moved out to go and live with her.'

'What?' The hurt was apparent on Megan's face. 'He can't be. Dad wouldn't do that to me. To you.'

Homing in on Megan's first response, Patricia said, 'I'm afraid he already has.'

Stunned, Megan remained silent for a few minutes as tears dripped down her face. Rubbing them away with her sleeve, she said, 'Who is she?'

Trying not to laugh humourlessly, Patricia said, 'His secretary, Karen.'

Megan's eyes grew wide. 'You have got to be kidding me!'

'Afraid not.'

'But she's old!'

'She's three years younger than me.'

'Yes, yes, I know that she's roughly the same age as you, but I mean, why bother having an affair with someone the same age?'

Although Patricia had been wondering the exact same thing, she didn't say so.

'What's he thinking? Is he having a mid-life crisis?'

Patricia shook her head sadly. 'I don't know.'

'Are you all right?'

'I don't know that either,' Patricia said, her voice wobbly at Megan's unexpected concern. She'd been so sure she would side entirely with her father, irrespective of who was in the wrong.

'I'm going to get to the bottom of this. I'm going to see Dad now.'

'I don't think that'll be possible, darling.'

'Why not?' Megan stood, her chin jutting out, indignation written all over her face.

'Because he flew to Prague this morning.'

CHAPTER FIVE

Arianna held her head in her hands as if doing so might give her the answer to the physics problem she was having difficulty with. I hope this is harder than the actual exam, she thought, or I'm stuffed. She'd been at the library every day this week and still hadn't spotted that boy again. Maybe studying at the library had been a one-off for him. Just her luck. Stifling a yawn, she made the decision to work for another half an hour and then go home. She was starving. Focusing on the twinkling Christmas lights on the tree, she wondered if perhaps they knew the propagation velocity of sound through air versus water, because she certainly didn't. It was no use. She was daydreaming. A break would help.

Getting up, she stretched her legs and wandered over to the easels she'd seen when she came in earlier. She hadn't had time to read what was on them today, but had made a point of reading them each day since they started going up, hoping they might put her in a Christmassy mood. She used to love Christmas, but with her family splintered, it wasn't the same.

Denmark – in Denmark some give presents not only at Christmas but on each Sunday of Advent. How good would that be, thought Arianna. Five times as many presents. She read how Denmark had a Christmas TV series with twenty-four episodes. *What a cool idea. We should have something like that here.* The Danish ate their main Christmas meal on Christmas Eve after church. Hmm, she wasn't so sure about that. Right, no more procrastination. Back to work.

Nope. Blank. Perhaps if she studied another subject. She had just reached into her bag below the table to get a book on World War Two when the sound of two familiar voices made her freeze. Cleo…and Aimee. What was she going to do? She couldn't stay under the table. That was ludicrous. But if she got up, they'd see her. Where were they? She tried to figure out their position, but then she heard her name mentioned. 'Arianna would never have had the money to go. You're being too nice, Aimee. I don't really miss her, do you? You know what they say, three's a crowd and all that.'

Cleo. She'd always known Cleo preferred Aimee to her, but then those two shared details about how far they'd gone with guys, and they always went into town on Saturdays to go clothes shopping, whereas Arianna, due to a lack of funds and a disinterest in shopping, had declined too many times for their liking.

'I do sometimes. She was funny and also good at helping with homework.'

The swot in Arianna felt a warm glow at the last remark until she heard Cleo say, 'Yeah, that's all she was good for, though, doing our homework for us.'

Arianna fought back tears as she shoved her physics books into her bag, hearing only one last bitchy remark from Cleo before she put sufficient distance between them so as not to be in earshot. 'But seriously, when is she going to get some new clothes? Did you see the state of her shoes today? I'm sure they're last year's.'

Wiping a hand across her tear-streaked cheeks, Arianna lunged for the door, hoping they hadn't seen her. Or had they seen her and were being intentionally nasty? Surely no one was that mean? She almost fell through the exit in her haste to get away from them and their horrible comments, and as a result bumped into someone coming in. 'Sorry,' she began, looking up from under her fringe. It was him. That boy. He smiled at her. She tried to smile back, but realising she was still too upset from her recent non-encounter with Cleo and Aimee, and she probably wasn't looking her best, she grew embarrassed, muttered a quick 'hi' and fled.

Star, who had witnessed the whole exchange, muttered, 'The winds of change.' Then she wandered away humming softly to herself.

Walking home, Arianna berated herself over her stupidity. She'd waited at the library the past few days to see if he turned up and now she'd blown it. He'd smiled at her, though. That had to mean something. She couldn't decide whether the brief meeting with him was a good thing or a bad thing, given the state she'd been in. Maybe he hadn't noticed. Boys weren't very observant about those things, were they?

Opening the door, Arianna crept into the hall. She didn't want her mum to see she'd been crying. She studied herself in the mirror. Great, she looked an absolute sight. Her puffy, swollen cheeks must have looked really attractive to X. She'd decided to call him X, since she didn't know his name.

Freshened up, Arianna went to let her mum know she was home. She heard her before she saw her.

'No, I'm not telling her. You can do your own dirty work, you useless... You owe her that much. No, I won't...'

'Mum?' Arianna said, concerned.

'Hi, love. How's your day been?' her mum asked, her voice overly jolly, as if she were putting it on.

'Not bad,' Arianna lied. Her mum had enough on her plate, without listening to her problems. 'Who's on the phone?'

'Your dad.'

'Really?' She perked up. 'Can I speak to him?'

'Of course,' her mum said, although Arianna noted she handed her the phone somewhat reluctantly.

'Hey, Dad. How are you? It's been ages!'

Arianna listened to her dad for a few minutes whilst she caught up on his news. He told her he'd been working loads and was up for a promotion. She told him how much studying for her exams sucked, but how she hoped to do not too badly in the mocks.

'I've got you a great Christmas present. You're going to love it.'

'Yeah?'

'Yeah.'

'So what day will you get here?' Arianna asked.

Was she wrong or was there an almost imperceptible delay before her father answered?

'Well, that's the thing. I'm not going to make it home for Christmas this year.'

'What?' Arianna was floored. Ever since her parents

had separated, her dad had always made a point of being home for Christmas, particularly as he missed so much of her life throughout the year. 'Dad, they can't make you work. It's Christmas.'

Her father cleared his throat, then said, 'Actually, I'm not working. I'm going to stay with friends.'

'Ah, well that's OK. I didn't expect you to stay with us. You always stay in the Hawksmeade Hotel, anyway. Where do your friends live?'

Again that hesitation. 'Nassau.'

'Nasser? Where's that?' Arianna had never heard of it.

'NassAU, Bahamas,' her father said uncomfortably.

Her voice cracking, Arianna finally managed to say what her brain had been trying to formulate. 'You mean you're choosing to go and visit friends in the Bahamas rather than come and see me for Christmas?'

'Arianna, it's not like that. That makes it sound…'

'Selfish? You're right, Dad, it does.' She slammed down the phone and burst into noisy tears as her mum slipped an arm around her shoulder and let her cry it all out.

'Hey, Evan, mine's a Tennent's when you've got a second,' shouted one of the regulars, his five-pound note already gracing the bar.

Evan wiped a wet cloth along the sticky bar, rinsed it under the tap, dried his hands, then grabbed a fresh pint glass and poured the man his drink. As he set it in front of him, he saw the time was 5.55. Great. Five minutes until the end of his shift. Maybe he'd drop into the library on the way home for the Christmas book session. He'd enjoyed the last one.

. . .

'So, have you all read *A Christmas Carol*?' Star asked the assembled audience of around twenty-five men and women.

Lots of nods, some shaking of heads.

'Who has read it this year? A show of hands, please.'

About ten or twelve hands shot up.

'And how many of you have read it more than once?'

This time fewer hands.

'And who reads it every year?'

Two women and one man put their hands up.

'And last but not least, who has never read it?'

Five hands.

'Right, well, you're in for a treat tonight. We'll start with reading an excerpt from it and then the floor will be open for questions about the text.' Star opened her copy and thumbed through until she found the passage she was looking for.

'That's me home,' said Evan, as he locked the door behind him and entered the living room. His family sat before him: Louise on the couch, Ryan and Georgia on the carpet, all watching TV. Some animated film he hadn't seen. Georgia and Ryan barely acknowledged him, whereas Louise raised her head to accept a kiss from him.

'Did you go to the library on the way home?' Louise asked.

'I did. It was really good. I haven't read *A Christmas Carol* since I was about twelve, but it's made me want to reread it. I think I can probably download it for free now. Classics are free, aren't they?' he asked his children.

Georgia shrugged as if she had no idea. Ryan looked at

him as if he were a moron for not knowing. 'Yes, they're free.'

Evan was pleasantly surprised that Ryan knew. He didn't have his son down as a reader of the classics.

'We got an invitation through for Tina and Gerry's party.'

Evan exhaled audibly.

'I've already texted her to say we can't make it this year,' said Louise, anticipating his reply.

'Thanks,' said Evan.

Tina and Gerry's parties were legendary. Often fancy-dress affairs, always oodles of champagne and Waitrose canapés, and Tina cooked a delicious three-course meal, and they all exchanged fabulous Secret Santa gifts, but the proviso was they couldn't spend any more than fifty pounds. Fifty pounds! When you thought about it, it was ludicrous. Fifty pounds on a frivolous gift for a daft party. Times two. Naturally he and Louise had to buy a gift each, so a hundred quid. Evan considered how much food he could buy his family with that sum of money at the discount supermarkets he'd begun frequenting since his financial decline. This year he didn't even have money to buy Louise a present, or she him, never mind a gift just for the sake of it. Plus they always took several bottles of wine and champagne, as well as forking out for the fancy-dress costumes, although perhaps they'd still have some of those in the attic. In any case, he was glad Louise had declined the invitation. The extra expense made it a non-starter. That was three years in a row they'd had to make their excuses, and only once wasn't down to financial penury. They'd be lucky to get an invite next year. Tina and Gerry's party was quite the hot ticket in their part of the world. If they hadn't been such good friends their invitations would probably have stopped long ago. Plus, there was no chance of Evan and Louise being able to extend an invitation to anyone these days. People expected invitations to be reciprocal, and they weren't currently in a position to host a party.

'Dad.' Georgia perched on the arm of his chair. 'Can I have a new top for Charlotte's party?'

Evan exchanged a look with Louise.

'Georgia. We've talked about this, honey,' Louise said. 'I'll rejig one of your existing tops so that it looks different, spangly, Christmassy.'

'I don't want a rejigged top. Everyone will know.' Georgia stamped her foot in frustration and ran from the room.

Evan closed his eyes for a moment, as if by doing so he could shut out his problems. Then he felt Louise's hand on his shoulder. 'She'll be fine. I'll talk her round.'

Evan hoped so, because he couldn't possibly make their money stretch any further.

Patricia answered her mobile on the third ring. 'Hello?'

'Mum, it's me.'

'Graeme! What a lovely surprise. How are you, darling?' Patricia asked.

'Good. How are you?'

'Oh, you know,' Patricia replied vaguely, 'busy.'

'And how's Dad?'

Was she mistaken or was there a glimmer of reticence, an indication he might know, in his voice?

'In Prague,' she said, avoiding a direct answer.

'He's not, Mum.'

'He's not?'

'No. He's back in Hawksmeade.'

'He is?'

'He rang me last night. Told me you were getting a divorce.'

Patricia staggered, then, regaining her composure, held tightly onto a nearby chair for support.

'Divorce?' She tried out the word.

'Yes. What's going on?'

'What has your father told you?'

It turned out Megan wasn't the only one their father hadn't told about his mistress. Ian had cited Patricia and his having grown apart, fallen out of love, as the reason for the split. Well, that was partly true, she supposed. But trust Ian to have been sparing with the details, particularly when they reflected badly on him.

'Do you want me to come home? I'm in Taiwan at the minute, but if you need me, I'll come.'

Patricia thought of what a comfort Graeme would be to her right now. But no, he had his work, his travels, his life in London, just as Megan had hers in Wales.

'I'll be fine, darling. Your father and I need to straighten a few things out, that's all.' She didn't clarify if that meant before they could get back together or before their divorce. Divorce. Nice of Ian to tell her! Imagine telling their son and not telling her that was his intention! What an absolute…she didn't want to think about it. She didn't want to be one of those embittered wives who ripped up their husband's clothes and threw them into the street, but right now it was tempting. No, she could never be that person. But she had to get out of this limbo. Ian was holding all the trump cards at the moment and that had to change.

CHAPTER SIX

'Vic, I'm going to drop the kids off, then I'm heading straight into the office. I've made you some tea and a bacon roll.'

Victoria raised her eyes to him, mumbled something indistinct and slumped back under the covers. Tired, thought Daniel. I'll let her sleep, then.

'Oh, Dex wet the bed again last night. Do we have a spare waterproof sheet? That's the third time this week. Do you think I should take him to the doctor?'

Silence.

'Well, I might call Dr Sanderson, anyway. See you later.' He leant forward and kissed the part of Victoria's head which was protruding from the covers.

Daniel kissed his children goodbye, then put the car in gear and started the journey to his office. Maya had been clingy this morning. Sometimes he still thought she was too young for nursery. He knew she missed her mum. Victoria was there in body but not in spirit. If a three-year-old could notice it, then others would as well. Daniel's thoughts occupied him so completely he didn't notice the Christmas market tagged on to the end of Main Street, or the strings of lights which hung from every lamp post. By this point in December, he was usually full of the joy of the season, looking forward to kicking back for ten days' holiday and spending quality time with his wife and children. Unfortunately, this year things were different.

'You're twelve per cent down on last month's sales figures,' Daniel's boss, Craig, told him.

'That's because we had the spike last month with the Comal deal. Remember they took two months' worth of orders in one go?'

'Hmm,' said Craig, unconvinced.

Daniel declined to mention it was also because he had been working his backside off covering his two colleagues' territories as well, both of which had seen growth last month.

'We need another £50K on the books by the end of the month. Let me know by close of business tomorrow what you can contribute to that.' Craig snapped his Filofax closed and strode from the room.

Fifty thousand pounds. So, presumably Craig expected him to come up with half of that, since he was covering two territories in addition to his own. Where was he meant to conjure it up from? He hoped his colleagues in the three other territories had some good news to share which would lessen the burden. Daniel scanned the open order book, wondering if he could pull forward more than a few orders to this month. He'd worry about next month later.

. . .

At first, Patricia, who had just left the library for her lunch break, didn't notice her friend, who had her head down and was seemingly in another world.

'Hi, Marjorie. How are you? How's Kenneth? All ready for the dinner party tomorrow?'

Marjorie, looking nervous, said, 'Actually, I'm afraid we're going to have to cancel. We're having some building work done and it's not going to be finished in time. I really am sorry. I haven't got around to notifying everyone yet.'

'Oh, no problem,' said Patricia, dismissing her need to apologise by a wave of her hand. 'Hope the builders don't leave too much mess. What are you having done?'

'Er…em, just some bathroom renovations. But the whole house is covered in dust.'

Sympathising, Patricia said, 'I'm sure it will all be worth it when it's finished.'

Giving her a tight smile, Marjorie bade her good afternoon.

Strange. Marjorie hadn't seemed her usual bubbly self. Patricia's thoughts then turned to the shopping she was supposed to be getting in her lunch hour and she hurried on.

Dad doesn't love me. Arianna wallowed in self-pity as she sat in English class doodling on her workbook. *Well, he doesn't love me enough. Doesn't he know how difficult it is for me without him here? Doesn't he care?* Sighing to prevent herself from crying, Arianna scrawled furiously across the cover again. Mum had said not to worry, they didn't need him, they'd still have a good time. How? They had no money and Mum had no time, as she was always working. Some Christmas this was going to be. Yeah, it would be great to have nice things: a new phone, one that didn't take thirty seconds to load a page, or some books that weren't prescribed texts, or even a nice necklace, but ultimately all she wanted was time with her dad. The one thing he couldn't, or rather, wasn't prepared to, give her. Bitterly she wondered which of the three presents she'd get. Or maybe guilt would make him buy all three.

'Yes, Mr Jacobs, we'll have the order there by Friday latest,' Daniel reassured his client. Dexter kicked the back of his seat, whilst Daniel tried to convey to him, by holding up a hand, that he should stop. Riley was singing the Thomas the Tank Engine theme tune. Daniel, on hands-free with his client, drove along the road and lifted one finger to his lips to indicate Riley should be quiet, but his son mustn't have noticed as he carried on. 'I can't confirm yet if we can deliver the second batch to Bratislava before year end, but we'll do our best, and I'll keep you posted.' Daniel listened to his client's response, then exchanged goodbyes and hung up. Pausing for a second, he was about to remind his children they had to be on their best behaviour when he was on the phone, when it rang again. Daniel took a deep breath, then answered saying, 'Mr Peterson. How are you?'

'Daddy, I want to get more Hairy Maclary books and a book about bees,' said Maya, as she let go of his hand the instant they crossed the library's threshold. Her brothers followed closely behind.

'What book about bees?' Daniel asked, wracking his brains for anything she had mentioned to him about books with bees.

'Daddy, she has the same name as me.'

Then Daniel remembered it was a TV programme she watched. He didn't know if the book or the programme had come first, but she loved it.

They looked in the children's book boxes for Maya the Bee books, but couldn't find any.

'Can I help?' asked Star.

'Yes, please,' said Maya. 'I want a Maya the Bee book.'

'I would like,' Daniel corrected automatically.

'Do you want one too, Daddy?'

Trying not to smile and wondering if three-year-old girls were capable of being facetious, or if she was taking him literally, he said, 'I'm fine, sweetheart. Maya the Bee is for you.'

'Well, let me see,' said Star, tapping a finger against her lips. 'I know we have *The Adventures of Maya the Bee* somewhere.'

As Star riffled through the book boxes, Daniel's phone vibrated in his trouser pocket. Star looked up at him.

'Sorry…work. Dex, can you stay here with Maya and Roo whilst I take this call outside, please?'

'Yessir!' Dexter loved his role as honorary adult.

When Daniel returned five minutes later, Maya was sitting beside Star, who was reading to her.

'Sorry about that,' Daniel apologised.

'You seem to have your hands full.'

'They do keep me busy,' he said, smiling at his children. 'I could be doing with a nanny,' he joked.

'Well, perhaps not a nanny, but a babysitter or childminder can ease the load when you're working,' suggested Star.

'Childminder. Babysitter. That's not a bad idea,' said

Daniel, deep in thought. 'Could I advertise on your board?'

'Of course. Let me get you something to write on.'

Daniel ruminated on the many ways in which having extra childcare might free him up to do other things, essential family things. Who knew, perhaps it would allow him some time with Victoria too. Then they could try to figure out what was wrong with her.

'Here you go.' Star passed Daniel a pen and paper. 'Why don't you make your ad and I'll keep an eye on these three for you?'

Daniel shot her one of his, of late, all-too-rare smiles and turned to the task at hand. Trying not to bite the top of the pen, a habit he adopted when concentrating, he finally wrote in his neat script, *Babysitter wanted for 3 children – girl, aged 3, boys, aged 5 and 8. Good pay. References required.* Then he left his mobile for any interested parties to call.

'How does that look?' he asked Star.

'Perfect.'

'I hope so. My wife's not very well at the minute and any help would be welcome.' Then realising he'd confided in an almost total stranger without meaning to, he coughed and said, 'Right, kids, let's go. Shepherd's pie for dinner.' And with that, Daniel rounded up his brood and led them out of the library.

'Did you enjoy your dinner, Vic?' Daniel asked.

Victoria mumbled and inclined her head slightly. Daniel could feel frustration raise its head. He'd felt upbeat after leaving the advert in the library today. That plus the fact he'd had a call back from the cleaner he'd called the other night, who'd confirmed she did ironing as well as general cleaning, had given him a sense things were improving. But not with Vic. It was as if an impenetrable wall separated them. He knew it wasn't intentional on her part, but he didn't know how to reach her.

'So what are we going to do about Christmas then? Have you got any ideas for presents?'

Silence.

'Vic, talk to me. I don't know what else to do. I'm doing my best here. I'm worried the kids are going to have a terrible Christmas because I don't have time to organise it.'

She looked at him, her eyes dull.

'And I don't know *how* to organise it either. I'm not sure I even know half of what needs doing.'

His wife remained mute, so Daniel babbled on. 'I interviewed a cleaner last night. She seems nice and had really good references. I've arranged for her to come in twice a week. That should help. Vic–' Daniel placed his hand on her arm, his eyes pleading '–will you please let me make another appointment for you with the doctor? We need to know what's wrong.'

Finally Victoria spoke. 'Nothing's wrong. I told you. He says I'm just tired.'

'Vic, you're always tired. You don't look after the kids any more. You hardly speak to them or me. That's not normal.'

Again he was met with silence. When it became clear Victoria wasn't going to speak again, Daniel said, 'I'll do what I can. I've put up an ad for a babysitter.' Again nothing. Daniel left the room, closed the door behind him and retreated to his office. He sat at his desk, put his head in his hands and wept until he was empty.

. . .

Arianna was trying not to constantly watch the door. Both times she'd seen him in the library it had been between five and six o'clock. It was ten past six. He wasn't coming…if he ever intended to, today. Oh well, back to the Spanish Civil War. The words continued to blur in front of her, until a voice said, 'Here's a voucher for the new café.'

Arianna looked up. The librarian, Star, was standing over her holding out a leaflet. Scrolls – the new library café. She had noticed the area which had been cordoned off for over a year had opened for the first time the other day, and that readers were taking books off the shelves and settling into Scrolls to take a few minutes to themselves, but since she hadn't any money to join them, it hadn't been of any interest to her. She took the leaflet from Star and thanked her. If she could just finish this history assignment, then she could have a break, maybe try out the café before she tackled her physics past papers again. She couldn't help groaning thinking about them. She'd barely started when she heard Star's voice again, followed by a male voice. She looked up. It was him. Star was talking to X. Partially dissolved snowflakes covered his hair. Arianna looked outside. Yes, it had started snowing since she'd come in. She hadn't even noticed.

'Sorry, Josh, this computer doesn't seem to be working. Let's try this one here. Nope, how strange. There's only one other left. Hope we can get some luck there.' She headed for the PC next to Arianna's.

Arianna gulped. She tried to look away, but his gaze met hers. There was the hint of a smile playing on his lips as the corners of his eyes creased. Her cheeks flaming red, Arianna gave him a brief incline of the head and returned to her books. *Oh God, how am I meant to get any work done now?*

'Bingo,' said Star. 'This one's working. Oh, I almost forgot, here's a voucher for the new Scrolls café. Studying's thirsty work.'

The boy thanked her and sat down. Josh. Star had called him Josh. Josh. She liked that. Suited him. He was sitting less than a metre away now – only a computer separating them. Arianna spent a torturous half hour wondering what to say to him, if anything. He hadn't spoken to her, although he had acknowledged her. Surely if he was interested, even just in talking, he would have made conversation? Trying to turn her attention back to her studies, Arianna leafed through what she had done so far that day.

'That girl with the dark curly hair, wasn't she in here yesterday and the day before?' Patricia asked Star.

'Yes, I believe so.'

'She used to only come in every other day.'

'Is that so?' Star tried to keep the grin out of her voice.

Patricia jumped at the sound of her text message alert. 'Excuse me a second, Star.' Opening the message, she saw it was a reply from Ian. *Friday. I'll come round at 7 p.m.*

That was it. More than twenty years of marriage and those were all the words he could afford her.

'So do you fancy using your coffee voucher?' a voice asked.

Arianna glanced up. Josh stood in front of her, grinning. 'You look as bored with revision as I am. Can I tempt you?'

She wondered if the double-entendre had been deliberate. Her face flushed red again.

'Sure.' She tried to play it cool.

His smile was contagious. She picked up her bag and followed him into the library's café.

'There's a letter on the hall table for you, love.'

'Hope it's not another bill,' said Evan, as he unzipped his jacket.

'Doesn't look like one. Brown envelope.'

'Maybe it's an unexpected tax rebate seven years late.'

'I wish,' said Louise, through a mouthful of rich tea biscuit.

Evan turned the envelope over. University of Cumbria.

Ripping it open, he scanned the letter then punched the air. He had an interview!

'I'm Josh, by the way.'

'Arianna.'

'So how often are you here?' Josh asked her.

'That's as bad a line as "do you come here often?"' Arianna teased.

They'd been talking for two hours, during which time they'd found out they had a remarkable number of things in common. They both loved sport, took similar subjects at school, watched US crime dramas and didn't hang out with the cool crowd. She felt she could joke with him now. Rewind two hours and she was a red-faced, gibbering wreck, but Josh had a way about him which was very calming. He was so easy to talk to, not to mention easy on the eye, she couldn't help thinking. And he was talking to her! She almost had to pinch herself to believe it.

CHAPTER SEVEN

Evan could hardly contain his excitement next day as he finished his shift and headed to the library to prepare for his interview. He'd called ahead to book a computer for a couple of hours. Here at the library he could concentrate without any of the distractions at home. In just a few days' time he had an interview as an IT security specialist. For whatever reason, the letter had taken an age to reach him, so he didn't have much time to do his research. He wasn't worried, though. Preparing was what he did best. But that didn't mean he wasn't nervous.

There, finished for the day. Evan saved his file and stood up. The next Christmas book session was on today and he had devoured *A Christmas Carol* in one sitting. They had come to the conclusion that the Dickens classic merited more than one session, which he was pleased about. He had so much more input to give now he'd read it again, and many of the questions from last time made more sense now. As he descended the staircase he heard one of the librarians say, 'We'll have to cancel the book group.

Star phoned to say her car's broken down and she won't make it in time. Unless you can stay behind?'

'I can't. It's our wedding anniversary and we've got a table booked at Moriarty's.' Moriarty's was the most exclusive restaurant in town.

'I wonder if we can reschedule,' the other librarian said.

Evan, feeling daring, took the last few stairs, then said, 'I'm sorry to interrupt, but I couldn't help overhearing your dilemma. Maybe I can help?'

Evan explained that he had been present for the last couple of sessions and had just finished reading the book, so everything was fresh in his mind. The librarians looked at each other, then the elder shrugged, pulled her waterfall cardigan around her, and said, 'I don't see why not. It's better than having to cancel it. People will already be on their way here.'

'Great,' said Evan, genuine enthusiasm lacing his voice.

'I'll get you Star's things,' said Bridget.

The book group session went down well. There was much animated debate around the character of Scrooge, and this led into a discussion on actors who had played Scrooge over the years – Bill Murray coming a close second to Patrick Stewart. Bridget brought over some non-alcoholic mulled wine and some cinnamon Christmas tree biscuits which Jessica had baked. The Christmas crowd devoured them and chatted amongst themselves, whilst Evan handed out copies of the next Christmas book choice for discussion at the following week's session. By the time they all left half an hour later, Evan was in a great mood and looking forward to sharing his news with his wife and children when he got home.

.   .   .

Patricia had left work on time for once, intending to do some Christmas shopping. It was odd not to be buying gifts for Ian. Since their split she'd often stayed late at work, helping out, so as not to be alone in the house for longer than necessary. But today she had decided that had to change. She couldn't use work as a crutch whilst she sorted out her life. She'd pottered around a couple of craft boutiques, hoping to pick up something for her daughter, and had gone into the local independent bookshop looking for a travel guide for her son. He was going on holiday to Bora Bora next year and she thought they might be able to order her a book on the island, even though she didn't anticipate them having it in stock. To her knowledge, it wasn't a common holiday destination for people from these parts. She managed to select a few other items for Anne-Marie and some for the baby, despite wondering if it was unlucky to buy gifts before the birth. Her friend already knew it was a boy, and Patricia had been unable to resist the baby blue pullover and matching trousers with a navy boat motif. Pleased with her purchases and glad she hadn't felt as if she were running around trying to fit in everything at the last minute, she stopped for a latte and treated herself to a slice of carrot cake at the café on the corner, Crème de la Crème.

She always carried a book with her and although she had an iPad, rarely used it for reading. Perhaps it was the librarian in her. She preferred the paper version – the smell and feel of a good book. When she read a library book it often made her wonder what kind of person had read it before her. Did they have the same opinions on it as she had? She sat for a time drinking her milky coffee, nibbling on her carrot cake, watching the world go by.

As she walked home, she found to her surprise she'd

taken a different route to that which she usually took. Shaking her head at herself in disbelief, she discovered she was at the end of the street where Marjorie and Kenneth lived. There was a lane which cut through from their street to the back of the estate facing Patricia's. Rather than turn back, she wandered on towards the lane. As she drew level with her friends' house, which was on the opposite side of the street, she saw there were quite a few cars parked outside, and that their driveway had two more cars in it than usual. It still didn't click with her. Not then. As she thought of the work they were having done, she gravitated towards her friends' house. The dining room window was ajar, and the tinkle of laughter reached her ears. Hold on, that isn't Marjorie's voice, thought Patricia. Then she heard Kenneth address Marjorie and decided she must have been mistaken. What she heard next made her blood run cold. 'Karen, could you pass the wine, please, darling?'

She saw it now, all too clearly. The party hadn't been cancelled. She had been cancelled. Replaced, as if she meant nothing, by her husband's mistress. She'd recognise Ian's voice anywhere. Traitorous git. Marjorie. She was complicit in this. They must all be laughing at her. Where was the loyalty? She'd known Marjorie since high school. Everyone was taking Ian's side. Until recently she hadn't even known there were sides. As she ran the rest of the way along the street, tears spilling down her cheeks, sobs wracking her slender frame, she railed against the unfairness of it all.

'Lou, that's me in,' Evan called.

No reply. Funny. Lou should have been home ages ago. There had been lights on when he'd arrived back. She couldn't be out anywhere with the kids at this time, surely? Evan kicked off his shoes, hung up his jacket and opened the living room door. Sitting on the armchair nearest the living flame gas fire was Louise, her cheeks red from crying. His children were noticeable by their absence.

'Lou, are you all right? What's happened? Is it your mum?'

Louise shook her head. She pointed to the floor. At her feet, Evan saw a letter which must have fallen from her lap. He picked it up and read *Notice of Repossession*. His jaw dropped and his good mood evaporated. Every ounce of hope seemed to have been jolted from his body. This was it. This was the end. After all the fighting to become solvent again, this was where it all ended. Laying the letter to one side, he took his crying wife in his arms and hugged her hard. She wrapped her arms around him as if she never wanted to let go.

'Are you OK, missus?' a voice asked Patricia. She looked up, a vacant expression on her face. She had no idea of the time or of exactly where she was. She must have been wandering for hours.

'I'm fine,' she said. Then she added, 'Thank you.' She felt as if few people cared about her at the moment, so the least she could do was be polite to someone who was showing concern. Disorientated, Patricia tried to get her bearings. Looking around, she saw she was in Hawksmeade. How had she ended up here? She started to walk again, this time in the direction of home. She couldn't have told you, even if her life depended on it, what she'd been thinking for the past hour or so.

As she passed Blair's department store, she caught sight

of a shape in one of the windows. Who was that? Was someone replacing the mannequins after hours? Looking more closely, Patricia was horrified to see it was her reflection which had caught her eye. She looked haggard, old, deflated, lost and unkempt. Patricia prided herself on her appearance. Three times a week at the gym: yoga, body attack and Pilates meant she had a good body for a woman of fifty-two, and she took care of her skin too. Although not fanatical about it, she also ate healthily. The fact she had never let herself go, until now, made Ian's betrayal even more difficult to stomach.

Quickening her pace, Patricia walked home, her mind whirling. How was she going to face him tomorrow? One thing was for sure, there was no way she was meeting him at home. Too many memories. After what she'd witnessed tonight she wanted to be tougher. There could be no going back now. It was clear he didn't think he'd made a mistake. He had already introduced her to their friends, for God's sake. She wondered how many others would make excuses over the Christmas period, or simply not invite her to their parties, because they now had Karen down as Ian's plus one. No, home was out of the question. It had to be somewhere neutral where he couldn't bend her to his will, bully her into agreeing to things she didn't want to agree to. An advantage to loving Ian, yes, she realised she still did, was she knew his faults, and one of those was he didn't like it when things didn't go his way. She had to get her head straight. The time for being the woman scorned had passed. Now it was time to be strong.

CHAPTER EIGHT

Evan tried to be philosophical about it. A house was only a house, he told himself. And maybe, just maybe, if he got this job, the bank might give him the wiggle room to sort things out. He and Louise had spoken long into the night about what they could do – the worst case and best-case scenarios. Best-case scenario would be a lottery win – difficult since they didn't have the money to buy lottery tickets. Worst-case scenario was they lost the house. They had tried to figure out if they could buy a smaller house, but didn't think they would get another mortgage, given their debt. So they'd be off the housing ladder at the worst possible time and have to rent, which was throwing good money after bad, not to mention the upheaval, both physical and psychological for everyone.

'Daddy, here's the brochure for Disney on Ice,' Georgia said, handing her father a sparkly leaflet. He glanced at the family ticket prices, even though he knew the only way he'd be able to afford it was if it were free. Sighing, and feeling as if he only gave his daughter bad news these days, he realised he had to have the talk with her now. Again.

'Georgia, I'm afraid we won't be going to Disney on Ice this year.'

'Why not?' Georgia scowled.

'Because we don't have the money.'

'I've got money,' Georgia proclaimed. And with that she ran upstairs, returning a few moments later with a large purple pig which she upended, spilling out its contents. She did have money. Probably enough for one Disney on Ice ticket, but that wasn't the point, plus she could hardly go by herself. Laying his hand gently on her arm, Evan said, 'I'm sorry, honey. Not this year.'

Georgia glared at her father, then flounced from the room, leaving her piggy bank behind.

Please, God, let this interview go well today, Evan prayed.

'Mummy, are you sick?' Riley asked, as he jumped up on the bed beside her.

'No, darling, just tired.' Victoria managed a weak smile for her middle child.

'So why aren't you getting up? We all had to get up, and I didn't want to. I was very tired.'

Seemingly lacking the strength to muster a response, Victoria turned her eyes towards Daniel, who came into the room bearing a tray with buttered toast, a muffin and a cup of tea.

'How are you this morning?' Daniel asked. He was dismayed to see her eyes fill with tears.

'Roo, can you go downstairs, please.'

For once, Riley was compliant.

'Oh, Daniel, I don't know what's wrong. I just feel so

sad all the time. And what have I to be sad about? I have you and our beautiful children.'

Daniel took his wife in his arms, kissed the top of her head and stroked her hair, as he would have one of his children. It was all he could do not to say, 'There, there, it'll be all right'. He was doing everything he could, but nothing seemed to help. He was muddling through: washing the kids, dressing them, feeding them, taking them to school and nursery and after-school clubs, doing the housework, feeding himself and Victoria – the little she ate – as well as working full-time. Thank God for the new cleaner. Even after just one visit she had proved to be a godsend, but still it didn't fix things at home.

'Dad, Maya's annoying me,' shouted Dexter from downstairs.

'I'm trying to brush his hair,' his youngest shouted back.

'I don't want you to brush my flaming hair.'

'Dexter, we don't use words like that.' His moment with Victoria cut short, Daniel had gone to the top of the stairs and called down to his son. He hated that: hollering to each other like fishwives. A flicker of amusement passed through his brain as he remembered his mother had used that phrase. Dexter had been playing up the last few days. Come to think of it, Maya had been cheeky to him too this morning. She had made fun of the boys, said boys were smelly and naughty. She was three going on thirty. Was there a full moon or something last night? Daniel asked himself. When he got downstairs after kissing Victoria goodbye, at least Dexter looked sheepish.

. . .

Star noticed Patricia didn't have the same spark she'd had the night before when she'd left to go Christmas shopping. Her face was drawn and her long blonde bob wasn't as expertly styled as it usually was. She'd obviously had little sleep. Just as they were breaking for lunch, and hoping Patricia would confide in her so she could help ease the burden, Star invited her for coffee again, and was glad when she accepted.

'That chocolate muffin was made in heaven,' Star said. 'So, did you get much at the shops last night?'

Patricia answered as if on autopilot, rhyming off the items she'd purchased. Star fell silent, waiting for her to add something, anything, which might give a clue as to what was bothering her. Wrapping her hands around her coffee cup, as if to gain warmth, and strength, from it, Patricia said, 'I saw my husband last night with his mistress.'

'Ah. That must have been hard,' said Star, understanding.

'Well, no, I didn't see them, I heard them talking. And it wasn't them being together which upset me, although now I think about it, it should have done. It was the fact they were at our friends' house for a dinner party. A dinner party the hostess told me was cancelled.'

Star felt for her friend, for she now counted Patricia as a friend. She always felt that way about one of her charges, one of those whom she had chosen to help.

'That can't have been easy.'

'No, it wasn't. I thought Marjorie was my friend. I didn't realise they'd be picking sides so soon. And why pick Ian's? He was the one in the wrong. It just seems as if he's got everything and I have nothing.' She blew her nose noisily.

'You have Anne-Marie.'

'She's about to be too busy to have time for friends, if we're honest. Becoming a first-time mum at forty-seven is going to be a radical change. She'll be worn out, and I won't burden her with my troubles. It'd be different if she wasn't pregnant, but she is.'

'And you have me.'

'Thanks. I appreciate that. Thanks for listening. God knows, nobody else does.'

'And what about your children?'

'I take that back. They've both been very supportive, although I doubt either of them know their father is already circulating his new girlfriend to our social circle. It'll make it awkward for Megan and Graeme when they're home, because our friends all know them too. They've been going to many of the parties since they were little.'

'Well, at least they're there for you.'

'Yes, but they're not local. One's in Cardiff and the other's in London.'

'Hmm, that's not exactly handy, is it?'

Patricia gave a tight smile. 'And the worst of it is, I have to meet him tonight. I told him a few days ago I wanted to talk to him, sort things out, and he was supposed to come to the house tonight at seven, but now I've told him it has to be at a pub. I don't want him at home. It'll be too difficult. Too emotional.'

'And has he agreed to that?'

'Yes, although he made a song and dance about it. Clearly I've inconvenienced him, as it's on the other side of town from ours. It's as if he's forgotten we ever shared a life together, as if he doesn't realise the distress he's caused.'

Star nodded sympathetically. 'Well, if you need someone to talk to afterwards, you can call me, or you can drop by. I'm at Cherry Tree Cottage.'

'Oh that's lovely, right by the river.'

'Yes, I like it.'

They chatted until the end of their lunch break, then paid the bill and left. As Star opened the library door, she said to Patricia, 'Remember, Cherry Tree Cottage.'

Evan's palms were sweating as he parked the car in a side street near the university campus. Right. Briefcase, check. Tie straight, check. Shoes gleaming, check. No food in teeth, check. No dog-breath, check. Hair in order, albeit needing a cut, check. This was it. Heart thumping, he got out of the car.

I couldn't have prepared any more than I have, Evan told himself as he crossed the car park to the entrance. He introduced himself at reception and a smartly dressed young woman showed him to a waiting area at the end of a long corridor, where six other applicants were already seated. Interviewing was in progress, so that meant at least seven. He wondered how many people they were seeing. He surveyed his competitors. Four men. Two women. One woman younger than him, he guessed, three of the men older, the other two about the same age as him. He took out his notes in an attempt to calm his nerves and not feel intimidated by the competition, who sat around him staring into space, smoothing down their clothes or reading their own notes.

. . .

That went well, Evan thought. Better than expected. When he had seen all those applicants his stomach had churned. Too much competition. He imagined at least some of them had lots of experience, whereas here he was, a rookie, trying to get on the IT security ladder. He wondered what criteria they would use when deciding who got the job.

Arianna's phone beeped. *You have a new message.* Clicking the icon, her face lit up when she saw it was from Josh. She'd given him her number the other night, before they left Scrolls to resume their work. *Going 2 library l8r. U going? If so, wot time? J.*

She texted back, *4.30. C u der.*

Cool. B der at 5.

Arianna hugged to herself the knowledge that in just a few hours she would see him again. She couldn't wait.

'Hi!' Josh stood over Arianna, grinning, his mussed hair flopping into his eyes.

'Hi! Are we studying or having a drink first?'

'Let's work first, get it out the way. Then we can relax.'

Arianna liked the sound of that.

An hour later, with only a handful of words exchanged between them, Arianna set down her pen. 'I need hot chocolate.'

'I'd kill for a beer, but a can of Coke will have to do.'

Arianna laughed and followed him to Scrolls.

They found a table easily enough, ordered and sat down.

'I like it in here. Makes studying less painful,' she said.

'I suppose it depends what you're studying, or who you're studying with.'

Arianna reddened.

Josh laughed, in a not unkind way. 'You're pretty when you blush.'

Her colour heightened further.

'Not that I'm saying you're not pretty when you don't, you understand.'

Arianna smiled. 'Quit whilst you're ahead.'

He laughed. 'So, are you worried about the exams?'

'A bit. Physics, mainly. You?'

'Geography. When I chose it, I thought it'd be all capital cities and culture, but tundra and flora and fauna don't interest me.'

'I know what you mean. That's why I dropped it when I had the chance.'

'So, what you doing for Christmas?' Josh waved his hand, taking in the multitude of Christmas decorations which adorned Scrolls. Even though it had only recently opened, it hadn't scrimped on the tinsel front. Silver and gold garlands were entwined around the staircase both outside and inside, and the seven-foot real tree stood right in the centre. The thousands of needles it had already shed were testament to its provenance. Santa and snowmen tea lights, already lit, given the hour, graced each table. Yes, Scrolls had done its bit for the festivities.

At Josh's question, Arianna's smile vanished. 'Don't know yet. Probably doing something with Mum. How about you?' She hoped he didn't notice her deflection.

A slight frown crossed Josh's face as if he realised something was amiss but she didn't want to talk about it. He then regaled her with tales of the Lightbody clan and how Christmas was a huge deal in their family because it was one of the few times each year when all of them got together, as his uncle was a contractor in Namibia, but always came home at Christmas to see the extended family, plus his cousins lived in different parts of the country.

'So what kind of things do you get up to?' Arianna wasn't sure why she was torturing herself, knowing she was likely to have a very simple, not exactly fun-filled Christmas this year. She still hadn't forgiven her dad, who had been Skyping her every night, trying to get her to see reason – his words.

'Well, we always spend Christmas Eve watching Christmas films. I quite like it, actually, but don't tell anyone! I'd never live it down. We have a big bowl of home-made soup around ten, and then we're allowed to open one present before we go to bed, but I prefer to wait until morning. I like the anticipation.'

'Sounds great.'

'We like it. It's a bit crazy as there are so many of us, but we have a right laugh.'

They chatted until, with a start, Arianna realised it was half past eight. 'Oh God, Mum will be worried sick. Wonder why she hasn't called.' Checking her phone, she saw she had, seven times. 'Damn, my phone was on silent. I'd better go.'

'Do you want to meet up next week?' Josh asked, as they put on their jackets and he paid the bill. Arianna offered him money but he refused.

'I'd like that,' she said shyly.

'Great.' Josh's smile outshone even the sparkly Christmas lights.

. . .

Ian was already sitting at a corner table when Patricia arrived. She'd chosen to get there a few minutes late. Her nerves were jangling enough without sitting there by herself waiting for him to turn up.

'Patricia.' His tone was frosty.

How could she have been married to this man? How *was* she married to this man? Although not for much longer, it seemed.

'Ian.' Her own tone was cooler than usual. She took off her trench coat, then sat down and immediately wished she had kept it on, as despite the warmth of the pub, she felt a distinct chill.

'You wanted to speak to me.' Ian got right to it.

'Yes. We have a lot to sort out.'

'Do we?'

'Yes.'

'Such as?'

'I'd like you to come and take all your stuff out of the house soon.'

'I've taken what I need.'

Momentarily put off her stride, Patricia finally said, 'OK. I'll bin what I don't want then.'

Ian looked alarmed for a second then said, 'I might just double-check I've taken absolutely everything.'

'That might be an idea.' Steeling herself, she said, 'And I don't appreciate you telling the children a pack of lies about why you left.'

'They're adults.'

'Yes, which is why you owed them the truth. Why lie to Megan, but tell Graeme we were getting a divorce? And incidentally, thanks for telling me.'

'Well, it'll have to happen sooner or later.'

'Will it? So you want to marry Karen then, do you?'

71

Sighing, Ian said, 'I don't know, eventually, perhaps. Not that it's any of your concern.'

'You're right. It's not. But what is my concern is the money I'm due as your wife. And I'll protect any money that should be due to my children too, our children. In case you decide to have any more,' she said pointedly.

'What do you mean?'

'You'll see.'

The barman came over just then and asked what they would like to drink. After ordering, Ian repeated, 'What do you mean?'

'Our wills will need to be modified. Beneficiaries. Executors. That sort of thing.'

'I suppose,' said Ian after a time. 'Megan's not speaking to me, you know.'

'You poor thing,' muttered Patricia. She debated whether or not to let on she knew he'd been at the dinner party with Karen, but decided not revealing that gave her the upper hand. She had no idea where her strength came from, but somewhere deep inside was the urge to put the power back within her reach. He may have left and carried on with his life as if she had never been a part of it, but it fell to her how she would react. Behaving rationally was the best way forward, she decided. Taking a deep breath she said, 'I'm going to contact a solicitor in the morning to start divorce proceedings.' She saw Ian's eyes widen, and emboldened by his response, she carried on. 'After all, there's no point dragging things out, now you've made your decision.'

'Isn't it all a bit soon?' Ian asked, once he'd rallied.

'No, I don't think so,' said Patricia, doing her best to sit still and not let her nerves get the better of her.

Hijacked and not the man oozing confidence whom she had sat beside when she came in, Ian simply said, 'Right.'

Standing up, she said, 'Well, unless there's anything else you'd like to discuss, if you could clear out your stuff, I'd appreciate it. My solicitor will be in touch. Bye, Ian.' And without a backward glance, she marched out of the pub. Once outside, Patricia leant her back against the wall, took several deep breaths and tried not to cry her eyes out.

CHAPTER NINE

'Ah, I see our little bookworm is back,' Star said.

At the sound of her voice, Daniel turned, then eyeing Maya, said, 'There's no keeping her away. She loves books. I can't keep up with her. She's read all those I can pick up in the supermarket and she was costing me a fortune, so it makes sense to bring her here.'

'It does indeed. So, do your other children share her love of books?' she asked, inclining her head in the direction of the boys.

'Yes, but not to the same extent. Maya's only three and devours them. I have to read about six bedtime stories every night.'

'There are worse things.'

Daniel considered his situation and agreed. 'That there are.'

'So, did you have any joy with the babysitting ad?'

Grimacing, he said, 'Not yet. I have to say I'm a bit disappointed. I'd hoped there'd be more interest, or at least some. Maybe it's the thought of my three tearaways, and that's without having met them!'

'I'm sure that's not the case. When do you need a babysitter, anyway?'

'After school. There's an after-school club but it's only for an hour, and Maya goes to it too, even though she's at nursery, but sometimes I don't get home until late. Plus it'd be nice to go out occasionally.'

'Well, tell you what, why don't I babysit for you until you can get someone else? I only work part-time here, and it's not as if I haven't had any practice. I've been babysitting friends' children for years.'

'You'd do that?'

Star nodded and waited as Daniel processed what she'd told him. She could almost see the cogs whirring away inside his brain.

'That would really help me out. Would you be able to do Monday afternoon?'

'I finish at three, so yes.'

'Could you pick the kids up from school?' He told her where the school was in relation to their home. It was all within walking distance of the library.

'Of course. It's probably best if we walk, though, so if I leave my car at home, would you be able to drop me home later?'

'No problem. Right, I'll call the school and let them know you'll be collecting them. Thanks, Star. You're a lifesaver. I have an important meeting I thought I was going to have to miss, but now I won't have to.'

'Happy to help. Why don't you introduce me to the children, so we can get to know each other a bit before I pick them up from school on Monday? Let me just speak to my manager.' Turning, she went off to seek out Patricia.

Once she'd explained to Patricia she'd like to take her break now, and why, she was more than happy to allow it.

. . .

Evan sat back in the chair at the library computer desk and sighed. He hadn't expected to hear so soon. He assumed the university would send an official letter advising him if he had a second interview. He had felt so certain he'd made it through to the next round. But there it was in black and white: *Dear Mr Donnelly, We regret to inform you that you have not been successful in this instance.* After reading that, things blurred somewhat. How could he have got it so wrong? He'd allowed himself to hope. He'd given Lou a reason to hope. Thank God he hadn't told the kids. Georgia would have been badgering him already for a saddle for the pony he was to buy her, and Ryan cadging money for more computer games. Well, at least he was in the right place, at the library. He was trying to find the positives in the situation and there weren't many. He'd check to see if any new positions had become available in the last few days whilst he'd been busy preparing for the interview. How was he going to tell Lou it was all a non-starter? Feeling despondent, Evan bent his head and thumped the keys, searching for jobs and answers.

'Corinne said she was at Marjorie Dawson's party the other night and Ian was there with Karen,' Bridget said behind her hand to Jessica, who was righting a holly wreath on one of the library doors, which had gone askew.

'You're kidding! Oh my God, you have to feel for Patricia. I mean, it must be mortifying. I wonder if she knows he's already flaunting his relationship with Karen.'

'Probably not. You know what they say.'

'That the wife's the last to know?'

'Exactly. But she seems to be handling it better than I expected. Apart from the first couple of days…'

'Have you said anything to her about it?' Jessica asked.

'No, I'm just surmising. She looked dreadful at first, as if she'd been crying all night, but now she looks, well, normal.'

'Hmm,' Jessica said, unconvinced. 'Oh hi, Star.'

Star who had heard the exchange, smiled serenely, placed the books she had been carrying on the carousel and went upstairs to the computer section. She saw Evan straightaway. He didn't look his usual upbeat self. Something was up. 'I hear you rode to the rescue the other night.'

'Hmm?' He seemed distracted.

'Yes, you stepped in to help out with the Christmas book session when my car broke down.'

'Ah, yes. I enjoyed it. How's your car?'

'It needs a new starter motor, but the garage has given me a replacement car in the meantime. I'm glad you had fun hosting the group, because there were quite a few people who said they liked the way you presented it.'

'Really?'

'Yes. And, if you have time this afternoon and would like to help, you'd be doing me a favour.'

'I didn't realise the book group was on today. If you think I could be of some use, I'm more than happy to help.'

'Yes, we decided we'd do a Saturday session for those who can't make it during the week. And, thanks, it starts in half an hour. How about you come down to the desk in fifteen minutes and we can run through the layout and questions?'

'Sounds good.'

.   .   .

Evan hadn't been able to help a smidge of pride surfacing at Star's remarks. As she left, he felt a tiny pinprick of joy amidst the anguish and uncertainty which lay ahead for him and his family.

The staff had already decorated the library for Christmas, but it was such a big building that the few decorations which adorned it got lost in the hordes of books. Star would do her best to improve upon the current lacklustre decorations. She had nothing to do tonight after the book group, anyway. Actually, that gave her an idea for another masterclass. She hoped Patricia would support it.

Evan enjoyed co-hosting with Star. They made a good team. Some of the regulars commented on it and also said it was good to have two people to bounce ideas off. He got talking to some of the participants too. A few alternated between the evening sessions and the weekend ones, depending on their schedules. Simon was an air traffic controller who found it helped him to de-stress. Giulia said it helped with her English – she was originally from Piedmont in Italy. And Raymond lived with his mum, but loved reading and came to the library to get some time to himself. Evan found it interested him why others came to the group and what they got out of it. At the request of some of the book group and Star, he read aloud a couple of passages. Lost in the moment, he was transported to the time the novel was written. Nothing else mattered. All too soon, though, the session was over. For Evan, that meant home to face reality and give Lou the bad news.

.   .   .

Star put her idea to Patricia the next day when she arrived. She'd already made lots more garlands at home, as well as knocking together some wooden Christmas scenes: the nativity, the three wise men and some Christmas trees, as well as stockings and scenes depicting children building snowmen. Some she'd had for years, but a few she had worked on over the wet October and November evenings to have them ready for the festive period. Last night she'd sorted through them all and today had brought them into the library. Those should help jazz the place up a little.

'So, you want to have a craft morning for under twelves where they can make Christmas decorations which they can either put on our tree or take home?' Patricia asked.

'Yes. The children will love it, and what better way for them to celebrate their links to the library and Christmas than creating something that can remain here year after year?'

'Well,' Patricia said, 'although the council pays for a decent tree, the budget for decorations is pretty meagre, so any donations of any kind are always welcome. Plus, I agree, the children will love it. When were you thinking?'

Star outlined her plans, then said, 'And I thought we could help get into the spirit of things a bit more by dotting these around the place.' She bent down and removed several bags of her home-made decorations from beneath the counter.

'I was wondering what those were,' said Patricia as she handled a scene with wooden angels singing from song sheets. 'They're beautiful.' She turned the tiny handle and the angels spun around. 'Where did you get these? I'd love one for my house.'

'I make them,' Star said.

'You made this!'

'Yes, it's a hobby of mine. Second job, really,' she joked.

'It's fabulous. You're very talented. I once made a wooden cheeseboard in woodwork class. That's as far as my talents go, and even then it wasn't much good.'

'Ah, we all have different gifts,' Star said modestly.

'Have you ever tried to sell any?'

Star shook her head.

'Why not? They're amazing,' Patricia said as she examined the intricate detail. 'Are those actual words etched onto the song sheets?'

Star nodded.

'Unbelievable, and yes, of course you can put them up, and these garlands are beautiful. I'd love some for my staircase at home. I like what the café has done with theirs, don't you?'

'Yes, although I think white garlands would have worked better than silver, with the colour of the building.'

'Right. Well, you obviously know what you're doing, so I'll leave you to it.'

Star took her at her word and once the library was quiet, she started to decorate with gusto, humming 'Jingle Bells' as she worked.

CHAPTER TEN

Evan laid the *Telegraph* to one side and picked up the next newspaper, scanning the Situations Vacant section. There were so few new jobs out there. He could almost recite the vacancies from memory. He felt as if he was letting everyone down. Louise, as ever, had been supportive when he had told her he hadn't got the job, but it killed him that she was working a crazy number of hours and still they couldn't get out of this rut. He too was working as many hours at the pub as he could, even though he was starting to hate it. Unfortunately, apart from in the run-up to Christmas, he wasn't being offered many hours. He'd have to start looking for just any job soon. Well, he supposed in accepting bar work he'd already done that, but permanently. That would be saying goodbye to any potential career prospects or ambition he might still have. He'd go and work in a call centre if he could. But he didn't have the experience, and as he was overqualified, they wouldn't want him, as they'd know he'd leave at the first sign of a decent job, one more fitting to his skills. Hoping by the time he came back, the job sites he was about to search on would have conjured up the perfect position for him, he went outside to call his mum, who was always ready to dispense solid advice, and lend a sympathetic ear.

'Did you see the new post advertised today?' Jessica asked Bridget.

Her friend nodded. 'Yes, I was quite surprised. I had no idea we were looking for staff.'

'I know. I thought they'd have offered us more hours first. I wonder if Patricia knew.'

'Of course she knew. She's the manager. But it's a technical post, not just a librarian role.'

'That's true. I suppose we do need a computer specialist. What I know about computers could be written on the back of a postage stamp!'

Bridget laughed. 'You and me both!'

'Wonder what the new person will be like.'

'I guess we'll have to wait and see.'

Evan, who had been standing waiting to take books out, and whom they hadn't noticed, as their backs were to him, had overheard everything. Computer specialist? I wonder…

That afternoon, Star left the library and walked the short distance to Daniel's children's school. Maya stayed at the after-school club until her brothers finished at three forty-five, so Star spoke to one of the teachers when she arrived, who led her to an area where the children were waiting for her.

'How are we all today? Did you enjoy nursery, Maya?'

'Yes. I painted a big dinosaur – it was green, blue and lellow.'

'Ah, yellow's my favourite colour.'

'I painted it lellow, because my T-shirt is lellow today.'

'That's a very good reason.'

'What about you, Riley, what did you do today?'

Taking her hand, Riley replied, 'We made peppa mashy snowmen. Mine had a blue hat and black eyes and red buttons.'

'Sounds wonderful. A papier mâché snowman. Where is he? Are you taking him home?'

Riley shook his head. 'He's too big. Daddy will need to bring the car for him.'

'Well, your snowman will be right at home at the moment, won't he, with all this snow outside.'

Riley nodded, and Star turned to Dexter, who was standing a little distance away, with a sullen look on his face.

'And what about you, Dexter? What did you get up to today?'

A look of alarm crossed his face, then he said, 'Nothing.'

'Nothing? You must have done something.'

'The usual. Just stuff.' He fidgeted as he spoke to her.

'And did you do any Christmas-related stuff?'

'Well, we did help Miss Scobie decorate the tree.'

'Oh that sounds like fun. And who got to put the star on top?'

'I did, because I'm the tallest,' Dexter said proudly.

'You certainly are tall. You're almost as big as me.'

This seemed to please Dexter. 'Everyone says I take after my daddy. He's six foot three.'

'Yes, your daddy is very tall,' said Star, thinking of Daniel's lean yet athletic build.

'Anyway, shall we go? Do you all have your boots on?

We can tramp through the snow all the way home. Dexter can you take Maya's other hand, please?'

When they arrived home, Victoria was lying on the couch under a blanket. Star introduced herself and Victoria acknowledged her with a listless smile, the same smile she gave her children as they tried to clamber over her, vying for her attention and affection.

'Boys, Maya, why don't you show me where your toys are kept, and then I'll make your mummy a cup of tea.'

'OK,' said Maya excitedly, leading Star by the hand. As she was dragged away, Star cast a backwards glance at Victoria, who smiled weakly.

Riley was determined to show her his Thomas the Tank Engine train set first, but Maya was intent on showing Star her construction vehicles. Dexter hung back, then disappeared into his room. Soon the low noise of the music on his handheld games console could be heard.

Once Star had settled the children and they were happily playing, she ventured downstairs again to find the kitchen. After reading the list of instructions she found from Daniel on the worktop, she put the kettle on, then studied the contents of the fridge. Chicken goujons, mashed potatoes and sweetcorn for dinner. It was too early for dinner, though, so Star rummaged in the cupboards until she found some cups, teabags and hot chocolate. All that trudging through the snow was thirsty work.

'Victoria, how do you take your tea?'

'Just milk,' she replied, raising her head with apparent effort.

'Biscuit?'

A small motion of her head indicated no, and Star turned back towards the kitchen. Poor woman. She clearly wasn't well. No wonder Daniel wasn't coping. At least he had a cleaner now. That was evident. The place was clean, if a little untidy. She suspected the cleaner only came once or twice a week, so in between there was plenty of time for the house to get messed up again.

Star went upstairs and told the children there was hot chocolate waiting for them downstairs.

'Yay,' said Riley.

'Hurrah,' Maya cried.

Dexter followed his siblings down to the kitchen.

Hmm. Star eyed him thoughtfully, then took tea through to Victoria, who had just about managed to lever herself into a sitting position.

Star placed the mug of tea on a coaster which ironically read Happy Times, one of a set of six dotted around the room.

'Would you mind if I sat with you for a bit?' Star asked. 'The children are drinking their hot chocolate in the kitchen.'

She'd left them sitting at the round, country pine, kitchen table, sipping their drinks, with Dexter under strict instructions to supervise the other two, so they didn't spill any.

'Maya's very articulate for her age,' Star remarked. Again a weak smile from Victoria, who appeared to be putting all her concentration into lifting her mug to her mouth.

'And Riley is such a sociable little boy.' Nothing. Star continued. 'I take it Dexter is the strong, silent type, although he's clearly clever too.'

Star looked at Victoria, whose overly pale complexion and greasy hair belied the beauty which lay beneath. Star saw a woman trapped. Trapped by illness, trapped by fear. She'd seen it before. She could tell Victoria was too scared to face her illness, acknowledge it existed. Yet until she did so, she and her family would continue to suffer. Her eyes fell on a gold locket around Victoria's neck.

'What a beautiful locket. Is it very old?'

It seemed to cost Victoria to say, 'It was my great-grandmother's.'

'Ah, so it is old. Does it still open?'

Victoria nodded. 'But I can't…' She fiddled with the locket.

'Would you like me to open it for you?'

Victoria nodded again. Star knelt down beside her and with one click revealed its contents. Nestling inside was a picture of the three children, taken not long after Maya was born.

'Beautiful. You really are blessed.' For Star's powers to work, all she had to do was touch the subject. She patted Victoria's arm, then closed the locket again.

As Star stood up, Victoria felt a moment of lightness, as if a weight had been lifted from her.

'I'll just check on the children,' Star said.

Arianna waited. And waited. And waited. He wasn't coming. She couldn't believe it. Actually, no, she could. Why should she expect anything different? Men were always letting her down. First her father, now Josh. She bit her lip. She thought he'd liked her, at least as a friend. She'd liked him, and perhaps was beginning to develop feelings for him, but obviously he didn't feel the same way, or he wouldn't have blown her off like that, without even texting to tell her. That was the pits. Maybe he'd had an accident. Maybe he'd lost his phone. Yeah, right. Those were the kind of dumb things girls told themselves when guys stood them up. Arianna had walked up and down in front of the storyboards, reading and rereading how the Madagascans celebrate Christmas. The only thing which brought a slight chuckle was the fact they called Santa Claus *Dadabe Noely*. She liked that, although she did think it gave the impression of a Rastafarian, dreadlocked Santa Claus, and that was Jamaica, not Madagascar, anyway. *God, but my head's all over the place tonight. There's nothing else for it, I may as well study. The exams are only a couple of days away.* With that she turned her attention back to the history book before her, with renewed determination.

Daniel arrived home, a little later than he had expected. The meeting had run on longer than expected.

'Sorry I'm late,' he said to Star, looking harassed.

'It's fine. They've been as good as gold.'

Daniel's gaze drifted towards the living room, his thoughts on Victoria.

'Victoria's had some dinner. I'm just going to clear away her things.'

Before his children noticed he was home, and enveloped him in bear hugs and flung little arms around his legs, Daniel went in to spend a few quiet moments with Victoria. He was astounded to see she was sitting up, and from the remnants on her plate, had apparently eaten most of her meal. She had lost so much weight recently and had little appetite.

'Hi, darling.' He bent down and kissed her on the cheek.

'Hi, Daniel,' she replied.

This was almost more than he could have hoped for. He had had to tease every word out of her in the past couple of months, or was it longer than that now? The days tended to pass in a blur.

'I'll check on the children and then I'll drive Star home.'

'Daddy, Daddy, Daddy!' shouted Maya, flinging herself at his knees. Riley followed her example. Only Dexter stayed behind.

'Well, that's a welcome.' Daniel laughed, picking up his youngest and giving her a big kiss, then ruffled Riley's hair. Seeing Dexter standing a little way off, he said, 'How's the man of the house today? Have you been looking after everyone?'

Dexter's muted response was just what Daniel had come to expect from his mother. After settling the children again, Daniel told Dexter he was going to take Star home. He would only be ten minutes. 'Can you keep an eye on your brother and sister, and if you need anything go and tell Mummy?'

'Yes, Daddy.'

'Good man,' said Daniel.

Star told the children she'd enjoyed spending time with them, said goodbye and then popped in to see Victoria again.

'I hope you're feeling a bit better. I look forward to seeing you soon.'

'Thank you.'

Daniel watched as Victoria smiled at Star. It lit up her face and reminded him of how she had been before she had fallen ill. A glimmer of hope crossed his drawn face.

What appeared to be thrash metal emanated from Daniel's radio. He grimaced and Star said, 'You don't like it either? Would you mind if we changed it to Radio Four?'

'Not at all.'

Daniel flicked through the stations and soon arrived at Radio Four.

'Tonight's speaker is Professor Frank Donohue of the British Confederation of Psychologists. Welcome.'

'Thanks, Gordon. It's a pleasure to be here.'

'Now the subject tonight is a fascinating but delicate one, I understand.'

'Yes, clinical depression can be a severe and scary illness, not least because often the sufferer and their family don't realise that's what's wrong.'

'Yes, that must be difficult and place a great strain on relationships, and not only those between husband and wife.'

Daniel listened. And listened. And the more he listened, the more he realised they could have been talking about Victoria. He wondered how he could have been so blind.

CHAPTER ELEVEN

'Are you sure it was Dexter?' Daniel asked, unable to believe what his son's headmistress was telling him. 'Yes, I'll be there in an hour. I'm about forty miles away at the moment. No, his mother can't come and get him. I'll explain when I get there.'

Daniel sighed and, not looking forward to the conversation, went in to see his boss.

'Daniel, have you got those figures ready yet for the Everbaum deal?'

'Not quite. Craig, I need some time off.'

'Time off?' Craig asked, as if the concept were absurd. 'When?'

'Now. I need to go to my son's school.'

'Can't your wife go?' Craig asked, not looking up from his paperwork.

'No, she can't. She's not well.'

'Well, if you must. How long will you be gone?'

'I don't know. A couple of hours, at least.'

Craig tutted. 'This isn't good enough, Daniel. We have a lot on this month before the Christmas shutdown.'

Gritting his teeth, Daniel said, 'I'm well aware of that, Craig, but I have to look after my family too. There's been an incident at the school and I need to go and deal with it.'

Looking a tad chastened, Craig said, 'OK. I suppose you can go, but make sure you work from home later today.'

'That'll be fine,' Daniel said, leaving the room quickly in case he said something he regretted. Everything he did for this company, all the extra hours he put in, with never a thank you, and he was getting all sorts of hassle from Craig over having to take a few hours off. He'd never taken time off work to deal with the kids. Ever since Victoria had been incapable of looking after the children, he'd even managed the kids' dental appointments so they were at the weekend, and he could take them without impacting his work. Fuming, he headed for his car, aware he needed to calm down before he reached the school.

Patricia stood in the queue for the cash machine, listening to the strains of 'O Come All Ye Faithful' from the nearby carol singers. There were queues for everything at the minute: the one downside to Christmas, she always thought, although this year there was more than one. Finally she reached the front of the queue, opened her purse, took out her bank card and slotted it into the ATM. She withdrew one hundred pounds, then glanced at the balance. What? That couldn't be right. The account appeared to have been practically cleaned out. There should have been almost two thousand pounds in it. Had she been the victim of fraud? Panicking, she went inside the bank.

. . .

Daniel reached the school in fifty-five minutes, slung his car into one of the available spaces and tried to compose himself as he strode towards the school entrance. All the way there he'd asked himself what had been going through his eldest's mind, what had possessed him to do it.

'I'm here to see Mrs McCluskey. She's expecting me. Daniel Fairchild.'

The secretary told him to take a seat. A few minutes later, the headmistress came out and showed Daniel into her office. 'Rita, could you send for Dexter, please? Would you like tea or coffee, Mr Fairchild?'

The secretary acknowledged her boss' request with a slight nod.

'Coffee, please.'

'Two coffees, as well, Rita.' Once her secretary left the room, Mrs McCluskey got right to the point. 'As I said on the phone, Mr Fairchild, Dexter has been disciplined today for striking a pupil.' Holding up a hand to stem his questions for now, she continued, 'Now, whilst I know boys will be boys, the reason I called you is because the boy in question required stitches.'

'Stitches?'

'Yes, a member of staff took him to the cottage hospital.'

'Dexter wouldn't hurt a fly. How could he hit someone so hard he required stitches?'

'Well, I think the fact he hit him over the head with a chair might have something to do with it.'

Daniel was aghast. Dexter. His Dexter. It didn't make sense. Dexter was one of the gentlest, least confrontational children he knew.

'Before we call Dexter in, I wanted to ask if you can think of any reason for his behaviour. Has he been acting up recently? Are there any issues at home which might have any bearing on what's happened?'

Daniel's thoughts were in turmoil. He didn't want to betray his wife. She'd be mortified if she knew he was discussing her health with anyone without her knowledge, but it was the only reason he could think of for Dexter acting out of character. His mum hadn't been there for him of late, through no fault of her own. Trying to choose his words carefully, Daniel explained to the headmistress about Victoria's illness.

'Star, have you got a minute?' Evan asked.

'Of course,' she said, smiling at him, her hands full of materials she had bought for the Christmas decoration masterclass.

'I understand there might be a job coming up here.'

Star, who had heard the same thing herself only this morning, said, 'That's right. An IT manager/librarian role. Are you interested?'

'Well, yes. I've really enjoyed the Christmas sessions I've been at and held with you, and I trained as an IT security specialist, but I know quite a bit about general IT too. Plus, cards on the table, I don't seem to have any luck getting the jobs I'm actually qualified for. I was wondering what qualifications they're looking for and how much it would cost to retrain – again.'

'Well, yes, to be a librarian you have to do exams, but I'm not sure what they're looking for from the IT manager. From memory, I think the job description said it was a dual role – part librarian, part IT guru. If I recall correctly, you'd need a degree as a minimum. I take it you have an IT-related degree?'

'Yes, although I don't have a qualification in librarianship.'

'That might not rule you out, though. I don't know how much weight my tuppence worth will carry, but if you'd like, I'll put in a good word for you. You've been a natural with the library's customers.'

In the past, Evan had been too proud to accept help when applying for jobs, wanting always to make his own way, do everything on his own merit, but his options were limited, so he said, 'I'd appreciate that.'

'No problem. I'll see what I can do.'

As she turned her back on him, Star almost rubbed her hands in glee. Things were taking a step in the right direction.

Patricia stood outside the bank, still in shock. The teller had gone to get the manager as Patricia hadn't believed her. She still couldn't take in what he had told her. Ian had severely depleted their funds, for what purpose she didn't know. What she did know was she wasn't having it. Fury coursed through her. Ian had always had the upper hand in their relationship, but sometimes underestimating someone gave them the advantage, and that's what Patricia was counting on now.

CHAPTER TWELVE

I'm sorry. I'm so sorry. My bus crashed and my phone was out of charge. Arianna had read the text from Josh almost a hundred times. She didn't believe him. My bus crashed. Yeah, right. Good one. He could have been more original. She ignored his text. She'd had enough of people letting her down. The only one who was ever there for her, whenever she could be, was her mum. Unfortunately, her poor mum worked twelve-hour days, six days a week.

When she got home the other night, Arianna had made sure she left her phone downstairs. Otherwise she knew she'd have been looking at it every thirty seconds, waiting to see if Josh had been in touch. Good thing she had. He'd texted her at quarter past eleven, when she'd been fast asleep, or as fast asleep as she'd managed, what with her tossing and turning. Why did everyone in her life, except her mum, let her down? Why was no one ever there for her? First her dad left, then her friends abandoned her, now Josh – the only good thing to happen to her in ages – was already taking the mick. What was it about her that made people decide to treat her like dirt?

Deep in thought, Arianna flipped over the pages of the Christmas countdown calendar her mum had bought her. Today was the Grinch. Well, she felt like the Grinch all right. She couldn't wait until Christmas was over. All she heard at school was talk of the Christmas disco, which she wouldn't be going to. She wasn't going to hang about by herself, was she? And if it wasn't that, it was what phone so-and-so was getting, or who was getting driving lessons, for those who were turning seventeen soon. She used to enjoy Christmas until her dad left. They used to have great Christmases. Even after her dad moved to Dubai, when he came back each year, her parents always tried to give her a great Christmas. Apparently she was too old or something for that to matter any more. You'd think when the rest of her life was dire, her dad would realise she needed this one event to remain constant.

Arianna tied her school tie in a loose knot, then picked up her backpack and shoved in her maths books. Thank God after today she wouldn't have to look at these until January. The first of her mocks – A level maths. Well, the sun was shining. When she didn't know the answers, at least it was a pleasant day for daydreaming and looking out the window.

Evan came into the library before his shift at The Dog and Ferret. He'd decided he wanted to do a bit more digging into what it took to become a fully qualified librarian and could think of no better place to do his research than in the library itself. It was like a second home to him. The kids were at school and Louise had already started work. He was aware he had been spending a fair bit of time out of the house recently when he could have been spending it with the kids, but he told himself it would all be worth it.

Star was talking to a customer when he first saw her. He raised his hand in acknowledgement and continued to the computer area. He had just logged on and was scanning through his emails hoping for some nugget of good news when Star materialised at his side.

'I was hoping you'd be in today,' she said.

'Yes?'

'Yes.' She held out a piece of paper.

Evan took it and saw it was an application form for the librarian/IT manager position.

'I spoke to the manager and she's happy to give you an interview. She was particularly interested in your IT background. Can you fill in the application form and, if possible, give it back to me today? You'll get an email soon confirming the time and date of the interview.'

'I don't know what to say. Thank you.' Evan's eyes sparkled with gratitude.

'You're welcome. Just get the job. My fingers are crossed for you.'

'You OK, love? You seem a little down,' Arianna's mum said to her, as she trailed a brush through her hair, whilst slipping her feet into shoes which had seen better days.

'Yeah, I'm fine. I'll just be glad when the exams are over.'

'How did it go today? Maths, wasn't it?'

'Yeah. It was a killer, but I think I've passed. Hope so.'

'I'm sure you have. You're a very bright girl.' Her mum slung an arm around her neck and kissed her on the cheek. 'My girl. Love you. Now I've got to run, but there's macaroni cheese in the freezer you can defrost for dinner, if you want, or there's some home-made soup in the pot still.'

'Thanks, Mum.'

'You know I don't like you staying in by yourself.' Her mum hugged her again. 'Will you be OK?'

'Mum, I'm sixteen. I'll be fine.'

'OK. OK, I get the message. Did I say I love you?'

'Yes, you did!' Arianna smiled. 'I love you too. Now go to work!'

It was strange being home alone. She'd been at the library every night after school for months now. But today after that first mock exam, she'd chosen, what with the whole Josh situation, to go home and eat and study there. Plus she could do a little housework. Her mum had so much on her plate all of the time she was surprised she didn't explode. Arianna opted to have her dinner on a tray in front of the TV and then tackle her final history revision before getting an early night. If she didn't know it by now, she'd never know it. Having a decent night's sleep would do her more good than trying to cram at this late stage. Plus she loved history. Hopefully the essay question would be one she could really do justice to.

Her phone vibrated as she was sitting down with her macaroni cheese. Josh. Again. She ignored him. Wondering what to watch whilst she ate her meal, she flicked through the channels, then decided to watch a cookery programme which was starting after the news. She put the first forkful of food into her mouth then heard the newsreader say, 'And finally, we return to the scene of Tuesday's bus crash in Hawksmeade. The driver of the double decker number 47 Yoyo Bus has been helping the police with their enquiries, after he hit a bridge, causing considerable damage to the top deck of the bus. Passenger Martha Crawley, 67, said, "I got such a fright. I'm glad I was on the bottom deck, and how anyone up top wasn't injured I'll never know. We hit the bridge with such a thud. I did wonder when we took a different route from usual, but I thought it was a diversion caused by roadworks.'"

Arianna stopped listening at that point. Josh took the Yoyo bus. And from where he lived, it was probably the 47 he took. He hadn't been lying. The bus he was on had crashed. He hadn't intentionally stood her up. Reaching for her phone, Arianna scrolled to Josh's number and hit Dial.

Daniel was exhausted. He'd had to make a three-hundred-mile round trip today for a meeting and was now on his way back. Fortunately Star had agreed to babysit for him again. He'd felt relieved at being able to leave his children, and Victoria, with someone so capable. There was something warm and motherly about her. You felt you could put your trust in her. He yawned. *God, but I'm tired.* He needed to speak to Victoria in private – soon. But it wouldn't be tonight. He could have gone to bed right this minute, the way he was feeling. Checking the motorway signs, he saw he had only another twenty miles to go. Stifling another yawn he drove on.

The blare of a horn startled him and, with a start, Daniel realised he'd crossed two lanes and was heading for the central reservation. Yanking the steering wheel hard left, he pulled his car back into the lane, with inches to spare. Heart almost exploding inside his chest, Daniel, wide awake now, steadily pulled his car back across to the slow lane, and trundled along until he saw the sign which indicated the services were only two miles away. When he arrived at the Travellers' Break, his heart was still pounding. He'd given himself a real fright. If that horn hadn't sounded when it did, he would have hit the barrier. As he headed inside the restaurant to grab himself a takeaway espresso, he thought, *This can't go on.*

'Good to see you're looking a bit cheerier, love,' Arianna's mum said when she came home after her shift.

Arianna's smile would have melted ice caps. 'Hmm,' she conceded.

'Not going to tell me? Oh well, as long as you're happy, that's all I care about.' Her mum went into the kitchen to put a load of washing in the machine. When she came back through she said, 'I've been thinking about Christmas.'

Arianna's smile wavered and it was apparent from her mother's face that she could have kicked herself. 'Look, I know Dad won't be here, but I wanted to do something special, just you and me. I know I'm working Christmas Day, and there's nothing I can do about that. I've tried to swap shifts already, but it's not possible, but I thought we could start Christmas a little early. How about we go to the carol service on Christmas Eve? You used to love that as a kid.'

Holding back the comment that she wasn't eight any more, Arianna said, 'That'd be nice.'

'And it's not like I have to work all of Christmas Day. You'll probably still be in bed, enjoying the lie-in, when I get back. So we can either open our presents together on Christmas Eve after the carol service, or you can wait until I get back from work.'

'Why don't we do a bit of both?'

'Sounds good. And we'll still be having a traditional

Christmas dinner with all the trimmings, even if we're not having it at the usual time.'

It was obvious how much it meant to her mum to make her Christmas as special and normal as possible without her dad, so Arianna said, 'Michelle McGeehan had her Christmas dinner last year on the twenty-first, 'cos her family went to Tenerife for Christmas.'

'You see. We'll have a ball. Right, I'm going to make a start on that pile of ironing. Do you want some cheese on toast first?'

'I'll get it. You set up the ironing board.'

'Deal.'

Arianna's thoughts drifted back to Josh. Perhaps with the combination of her mum's concerted efforts to make her have a great Christmas, and Josh's presence in her life, Christmas wouldn't be a total washout after all.

CHAPTER THIRTEEN

'So I'm seeing a solicitor this afternoon,' Patricia told Star. They were ensconced once more in Scrolls during their lunch break. Patricia had just relayed the details of her conversation with the bank to Star. Funny, she thought, she could never have told Marjorie or any of her other friends this. She found Star so easy to talk to. Maybe it was because she didn't know Ian.

'I think you're doing the right thing. You have to protect yourself.'

'Exactly.' Patricia took a bite of her gingerbread cookie and continued. 'Who knows what he's planning to do with the money. Did he think I wouldn't notice?'

Star shrugged and let her go on.

'I mean, I know he dealt with most of the finances, but he must have known I'd look at our affairs – financial ones,' she said, suddenly flippant, 'now that I'm on my own.'

'Who knows what was going through his mind. The important thing is you know now and you can do something about it.'

Patricia nodded her agreement. 'Right, we'd better get back. I need to be in town to see Mr McGovern at three o'clock.'

'And I need to prepare for the masterclass.'

'You're so good at this sort of thing. You've no idea how glad I am you've taken over the reins from Anne-Marie for the Christmas event. I don't think I could have managed it, not with everything that's happened. And, at the minute, my Christmas spirit is non-existent.'

'You should look at today's storyboard. That will get you in the spirit,' said Star. 'St Joseph's Primary has focused on Latvia.'

'Latvia?'

'Yep. Did you know the first recorded Christmas tree was in Latvia?'

'No, I didn't. I assumed it would be somewhere like Norway.'

'Nope. Seriously, read today's board. It will make you feel Christmassy.'

This is one of the most difficult things I've ever had to do, thought Daniel, as his hand stilled on his phone. But necessary. Hands shaking, heart thudding, he dialled the number.

'This is the Samaritans. How can I help you?'

Daniel, trying to keep his emotions in check, said, 'I think my wife is clinically depressed.'

'Hi, Star,' Arianna said. 'You look busy.'

'Oh, I'm just fetching the materials for the children's Christmas decoration masterclass.'

'That sounds fun. Wish they'd had something like that when I was a kid. You should have an over twelves too,' she joked.

'Well, you're more than welcome to help. I could use an extra pair of hands.'

Looking at her watch, Arianna said, 'I suppose I could help for half an hour.' She was meeting Josh at Scrolls in an hour, and had hoped to get a little studying done by then, but on reflection a break might be a good thing. It would give her mind a rest, and the big kid in her really did want to make some decorations.

'Excellent.' Star handed her some glitter, glue and felt, as well as a bag full of coloured feathers.

'Thanks. You've been very helpful,' Daniel said as he ended the call. He looked at the phone numbers, addresses and website information he'd jotted down, where he could get further advice. Already he felt more in control. They'd beat this. He knew they would. But first things first. He picked up his mobile again and called Victoria's doctor.

Making the appointment behind Victoria's back was the second hardest thing Daniel had ever had to do. Now for the hardest thing. With a heavy heart, Daniel walked into the living room to have a conversation with his wife that he'd never considered might be necessary.

'I can't believe how many kids have turned up for this,' said Arianna.

'Yes, there's been a great deal of interest ever since the class was announced last week. But not everyone realised you had to book a place, and since it's Christmas we weren't going to send them away.'

'I suppose not,' said Arianna, twisting twine around the top of her bauble so it could be hung on the tree. After Star had shown her how, Arianna had been demonstrating to a group of older children how to do this successfully. The younger kids were drawing waves with gold pen on the various coloured baubles and the seven to nine-year-olds were attaching cotton wool to some baubles to portray snow, and cutting out felt Christmas trees to stick on to the plain baubles. The class appeared to be a triumph. The children were busy cutting, gluing, drawing or twisting. Arianna's phone vibrated in her pocket, and only then did she realise she'd lost track of time. Josh was already waiting for her in Scrolls. She texted back, *Be there in 5.*

Arianna slipped her phone back in her pocket and looked up at the sound of Star's voice.

'I'm glad you were here today. I haven't seen you for a few days.'

'No, I haven't been in,' said Arianna, although she didn't elaborate.

'Ah, I wondered if it was because I've only been working in the mornings. I've been babysitting in the afternoons.'

'Babysitting?'

'Yes, for that nice man over there. That's Maya, his daughter. She's three. And her two brothers. He was in a bit of a jam, and since no one had answered his babysitting advert…'

'What advert?'

'He asked me, a week or so ago, if he could put up an advert for a babysitter, but no one contacted him. So I said I'd fill in until he got someone.'

Cogs turning, Arianna finally said, 'I could do it. I could babysit.'

'You'd be interested?'

'Yes, I love kids, and I could do with the money.'

'Well, why don't I give you his number?'

Arianna took out her phone and tapped Daniel's number into it.

'Thanks for that. And this.' Her gaze swept the craft-strewn area. 'I've had a good time,' she said to Star. 'What about you?' she asked the little girl beside her, who said, 'Me too!' and held up the fairy she had made. Its wings felt like gossamer but had actually been taken from an old floaty scarf of Star's.

'I've got to go, though. I'm meeting someone at Scrolls.'

'It wouldn't be young Josh, would it?' Star's eyes twinkled.

'Yes,' Arianna said, reddening.

'I'll manage on my own. Thanks for your help.'

'You're welcome. See you tomorrow.'

'Good luck with your exams.'

'Thanks.' And Arianna set off in the direction of Scrolls.

'Hi.'

Josh's face broke into a smile when he saw Arianna, and he closed his phone.

'Hi.' Standing up, he said, 'What do you want to drink?'

'Hot chocolate, please.'

'Coming right up.'

Josh bounded over to order drinks and as Arianna studied him, she felt a warm glow.

Handing her a drink, Josh sat down and said, 'Look, I'm sorry about the other night.'

'Don't worry. If anyone should apologise, it's me. And I overreacted. It's all this stuff with Dad.' She couldn't believe she was telling him this, but it seemed right. 'Anyway, it's forgotten about. I'm sorry for not believing you earlier.'

'That's OK. I understand. But–' he leant across the table '–just so you know, I'd never stand you up intentionally.' He smiled at her, and Arianna's face flushed once more.

They chatted about the exams. Josh had one exam left. His school had started doing their mocks earlier.

'English, on Monday,' he said. 'I'm not looking forward to it. The only part I'm happy with is Harper Lee's *To Kill a Mockingbird*. I love that book.'

Arianna hadn't read it. She was studying *Brave New World*. 'I can't wait until the exams are over.'

'I know. It's difficult to feel relaxed and get into the Christmas spirit when your brain never switches off and keeps throwing mathematical equations and formulae at you!'

Arianna laughed. 'I know what you mean. I've been dreaming about the Second World War. It's been a bit like having a movie in my head. All I want is some time to do fun stuff, without feeling guilty for not studying.'

'I might have the answer to that. The fun stuff, that is. I can't do anything about the guilt. My brother called today. He has two tickets for the Snow Ponies tomorrow, but he can't go. He's giving them to me. I don't suppose you're free?'

Trying to keep the excitement out of her voice, in case he thought she was a total loser, Arianna said, 'I think I might be. Let me check my calendar.' A few flicks of her phone keys and Arianna said, 'Yep. That sounds like excellent revision for my music exam next week. Where is it?'

With the smile that Josh gave at her answer, it could have been on the moon for all she cared. By the time he had walked her home, they had made plans for travelling to the gig together, and as Arianna closed her gate, she couldn't help feeling warm and fuzzy inside.

CHAPTER FOURTEEN

'Craig, you got a minute?' Daniel asked, leaning his hand on the open doorframe of his boss' office.

'Can you come back in twenty minutes? I'm right in the middle of something.'

Fighting back a sigh, Daniel said, 'Sure.' *Sure, no one is busier than Craig. Yeah right.*

Returning twenty minutes later, Daniel knocked on Craig's now closed door, and waited for his boss to call him in.

'What can I do for you?'

'I need some time off.'

'You had time off last week, when you had to go to the school.'

'I know that. No, I mean like a couple of weeks, minimum.'

'Are you kidding me? This is our busiest time.'

'I know that, but...' Despite himself, Daniel's voice started to crack. 'Look, my wife's ill. Really ill, and she needs my help.'

'I'm sorry to hear that,' said Craig, not sounding nearly

as sorry as Daniel would have liked him to. 'But it's out of the question. We don't have the manpower.'

'Craig, you're not listening to me. I need the time off. I'm taking the time off. My family needs me. It's falling apart.'

An eternal bachelor and proud of it, Craig remained unmoved. 'I can't give you the time off, Daniel.'

'Craig, here's the bottom line. I'm taking the time off. Even if it means you fire me, I'm taking the time, as my family comes first. It has to. It hasn't done for so long and now we're in a mess. But I don't think it's in your interests to fire me, do you? So why don't you show a bit of human decency and agree to the time off and I won't have to quit?'

Craig stood with his jaw almost touching the floor. As far as Daniel knew, no one had ever spoken to him like that before, but Daniel's patience was all used up.

Chewing his lip, Craig was silent for a few moments then said, 'Fine. But I won't forget this, Daniel.'

'Thank you. Nor I.' Daniel left the ambiguous reply hanging. When Craig asked when he wanted his annual leave to begin, he was already thinking he'd start looking for a new job in January.

'I'll tie up some loose ends today and then I'll see you in the New Year.'

Craig was about to protest, but then realised, given what Daniel had said, that it would make no difference.

He grunted a 'Fine,' and then Daniel left.

That went well.

Patricia replayed the visit to the solicitor over and over in her head every spare moment she had. She couldn't help it. It was like a song stuck on a loop. She had no idea why she was persecuting herself in this way. The solicitor had advised her on freezing their bank accounts, and Patricia had been asked to make a list of all their assets and also all their regular outgoings. He had told her she was due half of everything. She had known as much, but she knew Ian would contest it. He wanted to divorce her, but she didn't know on what grounds. Her solicitor recommended she request a divorce on the grounds of his adultery. Would that go in her favour with the judge? Patricia had the feeling they were in for a long, dirty battle, and the truth was, she wanted none of it. She wanted life back to the way it had been before, the way it had always been, but she knew that wasn't possible, so she had to safeguard herself.

She was standing reflecting upon all this when she became aware of a presence in front of her. Looking up, she saw a man she'd never seen before, in his mid-fifties perhaps, with salt and pepper hair. The well-cut suit he wore accentuated his lean build.

'Can I help you?' Patricia asked.

'Yes, I'm looking for Arthur Miller plays, but I can't seem to find the drama section.'

'Oh, I'll show you. Plays are over here, to the left of Poetry.'

He followed her as she browsed through the stacks until she got to M within the shelves for American playwrights.

'Here you go. This one has *Death of a Salesman*, *The Crucible* and *All My Sons*, as well as a couple of lesser-known works.'

'That'll do for starters. Thanks.'

'You're welcome. I have to say *All My Sons* is one of my all-time favourite plays.'

'Interesting. I've never seen it, but I hear it's coming to the Grand soon.'

Was she imagining it, or was there a bit of a question in his voice? She wasn't, however, imagining the twinkle in his eyes as he held her gaze.

'Excellent. I'll need to find out what date. Wouldn't want to miss it.'

'Nor me.'

Definitely a frisson in the air.

As she stamped his books out, he said, 'Well, thanks for finding the plays for me. I'll be back again soon.'

Soon. She found she liked the sound of that. 'Look forward to it.' Had she said that aloud? 'I mean, happy to help.'

His eyes certainly danced this time. 'Thanks.' Leaning towards her, he said, 'And I'm looking forward to it too.'

Patricia's cheeks flamed, and before she could muster a suitable response, she discovered he had gone. Once she came out of her daze, she checked his library record: Leo Shriver, 14 Albion St, Hawksmeade. Local enough.

'Hi, is that Mr Fairchild?'

'Yes,' Daniel said, propping his phone between his shoulder and his ear as he tried to coordinate the pots and pans on the hob in front of him.

'My name's Arianna Gray. Star from the library told me you're looking for a babysitter.'

Turning the dials on the hob to the off position, and now giving the call his full attention, Daniel said, 'That's right. Are you interested?'

'Yes. I was wondering if I could come round and meet you and the children.'

'Sure. When would you like to come?'

'Would Monday afternoon, about two o'clock be OK?

And, I hope it's all right, but I asked Star if she'd come with me.'

'Perfect.' He reeled off the address and thanking Arianna for calling, he hung up, then gave a huge sigh of relief. Things were looking up.

'Anne-Marie, it's so good to see you!' Patricia hugged her friend as if she would never let go, then, mindful of her friend's burgeoning waist and unborn child, relaxed her grip. 'But what are you doing, crazy woman, hanging about outside? It's December, for goodness' sake. Let's get inside before we freeze to death.' Patricia pushed open the theatre door and ushered her friend through before her.

'It really is good to see you, you know,' Patricia said once they were ensconced in the warmth of the theatre café.

'I know. It's been ages. We've never gone this long without seeing each other. It was so easy when I was at work. Are you missing me?'

'You have no idea.'

'How's my replacement?'

'Lovely woman called Star. She hasn't quite filled your shoes in the friendship stakes, but I have been grabbing the odd coffee with her. And she's good.'

'And how are the gossipmongers?'

'Still gossiping.'

'So what's the goss?' joked her friend.

Torn between whether or not to tell Anne-Marie about her split from Ian, Patricia eventually decided to do so.

'I think I make up the majority of the gossip at the minute.'

'You? Why, what have you done?'

'Well, it's more Ian that's done something.'

'Ian?'

'We're getting a divorce.'

'What? You're one of the strongest couples I know.'

'We were. Not any more. Not since Karen replaced me.'

'His secretary? You've got to be kidding me! What a cliché. What a slimeball.'

'Yep, he's both of those things.'

'So when did all this happen and why didn't you tell me?'

'A few weeks ago. And you're eight months pregnant, and I didn't want to distress you. I'm only telling you now because I feel a bit better about it all. So much has happened in the past couple of weeks, but now I'm starting to draw a line under it and move on a little.'

'Good for you.'

'Right, enough about me. Tell me how you're doing. Any chance this baby's going to be an early Christmas present?'

'I bloomin' hope not. I haven't had my nesting instinct yet. The house is an absolute tip. Nor have I had the required period of relaxation to build me up for the great event.'

Patricia laughed. 'Stranger things have happened. Just be prepared.'

'Duly noted. I'm still planning on coming to the Christmas event, though. I'll make sure I pack my hospital bag. Are you all organised for it?'

'I think so. To be honest, Star has handled the majority of it. She's made it look so much more festive than usual.' Patricia didn't want to upset her friend by saying too openly that the library looked miles better than it usually did at this time of year, as Anne-Marie was the one who arranged it each year, but those decorations Star had made were pretty spectacular.

'And listen, don't think you can't talk to me about stuff. I'm pregnant, not at death's door.'

'Point taken. So, have you bought any baby clothes yet?' Patricia was keen to turn the subject away from herself. It was her friend's moment and she wanted to enjoy it with her, not bitch about her soon-to-be ex-husband.

As Anne-Marie told her about the babygros she had bought at an expensive independent baby boutique in town, justifying to herself the money she'd spent by saying they were the first outfits the baby would ever wear, Patricia found herself relaxing in a way she hadn't done since the news of Ian's infidelity had broken. She studied Anne-Marie. Pregnancy suited her. Her blonde curls boasted that shine which only pregnant women seemed to be blessed with. It reminded her of her own pregnancy when her hair had been a joy, but her back and legs ached.

'We'd better go in. It'll be curtain-up soon and it will take me ages to manoeuvre my massive bulk into the middle of the row. I thought baby brain happened once you had the baby. What on earth possessed me to book tickets in the centre of a row when I knew I'd be eight months pregnant?'

Smiling affectionately at her, Patricia linked arms with Anne-Marie and walked towards the entrance to the stalls.

'I knew they were good, but tonight they are awesome,' Arianna said to Josh, taking a selfie of her and Josh with his phone, then turning to take a photo of them again, this time with the band in the background. She'd never fancied anyone in a band before, but she had to admit Rob

Reynard, with his close-cut blond hair and gorgeous, cheeky grin, would have made her change her mind, were it not for the fact she was beginning to develop feelings for Josh. And Josh was real and within her reach. And he'd asked her here to this gig. He was looking at her now, his eyes laughing as he took her hand and they jumped up and down in time to the music. Standing at concerts was definitely much more fun than she imagined sitting would be. That was for the oldies. For now, she was imbued with the energy of youth, and she was determined to enjoy the experience.

'A fresh orange and lemonade for me,' Anne-Marie said when Patricia asked her at the interval what she wanted to drink. 'I can't even have a coffee. Well, I could, but I've had my one for today. I'm going to the loo. Be back in a minute. By that, I mean ten. It takes forever to lug this body about these days.'

'Stop exaggerating and get on with it, woman. I'll get the drinks.'

Patricia waited at the bar. It was a long queue, but fortunately there were several members of staff working. She was next but one in line when she heard a voice say, 'Fancy meeting you here.'

Turning, Patricia saw Leo Shriver less than three feet from her. He was wearing a long coat, jeans and a blue striped shirt. The ensemble suited him.

'What a surprise.'

'Leo,' he said. 'We didn't introduce ourselves earlier, Patricia.'

At the use of her name, Patricia raised an eyebrow.

'Your name badge,' Leo said, pre-empting her.

Realisation dawned. 'So you do like your plays, then?'

'Well, those I've seen and read, yes, but I'm no expert. Truth is, after speaking to you today, I checked what was on at the theatre, and thought this would be right up my street.'

Patricia couldn't help but smile. There was something endearing about Leo. He had an easy way about him. They chatted about the first half, remarking on how incredible a performance it was, even though it was opening night and one of the main actors had been replaced by his understudy, after falling off a ladder during rehearsals the day before and breaking his leg. Leo cracked a joke about show business' use of 'break a leg' meaning 'good luck', and Patricia listened attentively.

'Sorry I was so long. There were about twenty people waiting, and did anyone let me skip the queue because I'm eight months pregnant? Did they heck.' Anne-Marie stopped mid-rant when she saw Leo. 'Oh, hello.' She shot a questioning glance at Patricia.

Patricia, keen to dispel any untoward thoughts going through Anne-Marie's head, said, 'Anne-Marie, this is Leo. Leo, Anne-Marie. Anne-Marie's the deputy manager at the library, but she's on maternity leave at the minute.' When she stopped after that, Anne-Marie gave her a look to ensure she continued. 'And Leo was in the library today looking for Arthur Miller plays.'

'Ah,' said Anne-Marie. They chatted for a few minutes about various plays, but all too soon a bell signalled the end of the interval.

'Well, it was nice seeing you again,' Leo said. 'I'd better go and find my friend. He'll be wondering where I've got to.'

'You too. Enjoy the second half,' Patricia said, as she picked up her bag from over her chair.

As Leo walked away, Anne-Marie said, 'Now there's the perfect man to help you get over Ian.'

'I don't know what you mean,' Patricia said, though even to her own ears her protests sounded feeble.

'Oh, I think you do. I think you know exactly what I mean.' Anne-Marie winked at her.

'Thanks, Josh. That was just what I needed to take my mind off the exams,' said Arianna, as they got off the bus near her house.

'No worries. It was a bit of luck my brother couldn't go.'

'Yes, it was, wasn't it?'

'Oh, here,' he said, as they reached her gate. 'I got you a programme.'

Knowing they cost fifteen pounds, and although Josh's family was more comfortable financially than hers, they were by no means well-off, made his gesture all the more sweet.

'That was really thoughtful. Thanks. Are you going to the library Christmas party on Tuesday?'

'I wasn't planning to. Why, are you going?'

'Yes, it sounds good.'

'Well, if you're going that's enough reason for me.' Suddenly awkward, as if he had revealed too much, Josh coughed, then said, 'OK, well, I'd better get home.' He jerked his thumb over his shoulder in the direction of his street.

'I suppose.' There was a reluctance in Arianna's voice which must have decided Josh to act, as he then leant forward and kissed her softly on the lips. Arianna returned his kiss.

Oh my God, that was amazing!

As they broke apart, Josh said, 'Right, I need to go. Don't want to get grounded.'

'No, we can't have that.'

'See you at the Christmas party?'

Arianna nodded and Josh kissed her fleetingly once more. He walked away, then looked back over his shoulder and waved. Finding her voice again, Arianna whispered, 'You can count on it.'

CHAPTER FIFTEEN

Daniel had been surprised by Victoria's reaction to his announcement that he had arranged for her to see a doctor, a psychologist, in the first week of January. She had seemed almost relieved, as if the decision to admit something was wrong being taken out of her hands had somehow freed her. Certainly she was chatting to the kids more and participating in family life again. Daniel spending longer periods at home helped – in fact it helped everyone, including Daniel. He'd even been able to address the question he had put off for ages, about Christmas and how they were going to celebrate the day, and what presents they were going to buy the kids. Now that she appeared to have been roused out of her dreamlike state, Victoria did actually have some ideas on what to get the children, which was just as well, as Daniel had little clue. For Dexter, anything to do with Minecraft that he didn't already own, plus or minus a skateboard. Riley was going through a Marvel superheroes phase, and Maya would be happy with more books, although they also planned to get her a garage and some puzzles.

They'd bought her a doll and pram the year before, but they had lain in the garden shed for ten of the past eleven months, virtually untouched. She just wasn't a doll sort of girl.

It would only be the five of them for Christmas lunch. They weren't inviting friends, nor would they accept any invitations to leave their house on Christmas Day and join others. They weren't being selfish; they were simply rallying. For now, they had to concentrate on themselves, healing and protecting their family unit. Daniel felt a glimmer of hope that they might have a good Christmas after all.

'How are you feeling?' Star asked Evan, as he sat outside Patricia's office going over his interview notes.

Fidgeting with his tie, Evan said, 'Nervous. So much is riding on this. I feel like if I don't get it, then I'm basically unemployable.'

'Have faith. You'll be fine. Good luck.' Star walked off towards the exit, leaving Evan alone once again with his thoughts.

'Evan?' Patricia called, as she stood in the doorway of her office, his CV in her hand.

'That's me.'

'Come on in.' Patricia smiled warmly at him.

The doorbell rang. Daniel cast his eye around the living room to ensure there was nothing obvious for Arianna to fall over. He had asked the children to play upstairs until he called them down.

'Star, nice to see you again. Arianna, I'm Daniel,

pleased to meet you.' He extended his hand and Arianna shook it. 'Please, come in.'

Ushering them into the living room, Daniel said, 'Victoria, this is Arianna. You already know Star. Arianna, my wife, Victoria.'

'Nice to meet you, Mrs Fairchild.'

Victoria returned her greeting, and Star and Arianna sat down at Daniel's request.

Daniel wanted to know a little about Arianna, what she was doing, what babysitting experience, if any, she had. Arianna filled him in and explained how she wanted to work in Education. She loved children, but didn't have any brothers or sisters, although she had babysat in the past for her mother's friends' children.

'Well, our lot are a bit unorthodox but no more than other kids, I suppose,' said Daniel, pacing the room as he talked.

He explained what was required in terms of looking after them – their mealtimes, bedtimes and foibles. He also asked Arianna what hours she could work, and even though she couldn't cover all of the hours he needed, he decided he could work around that.

'So, do you want to meet the cherubs?'

Smiling, Arianna said, 'Yes, please.'

Shortly afterwards, the three children tumbled into the room. Maya tugged at her dress adorably, Riley examined Arianna with interest, and Dexter played his part well by being an angel. The little chat Daniel had with him following his visit to the headmistress' office the previous week seemed to have worked. Since then, Daniel had dedicated more of his available time to his eldest than usual. He knew Dexter's acting out was attention-seeking behaviour, and that they could only fix the issues if he spent more quality time with his son.

'Dexter, this is Arianna. Arianna, Dexter.'

Dexter raised his chin in acknowledgement.

'This is Riley, better known as Roo.'

Riley held out his hand, which Arianna shook as he pumped hers vigorously up and down.

'Roo, give Arianna her hand back, please. And finally, Maya, the only girl.'

Maya eyed Arianna with suspicion, then said, 'Do you like tea parties?'

'I love tea parties.'

'Daddy, we're having a tea party. Roo, can you help me bring the cups and cake, please?'

Arianna chuckled as Roo was led away by his bossy sister.

'So–' Daniel turned to Arianna '–do you think you'd like to take us on?'

'Yeah,' said Arianna. 'When do you want me to start?'

Evan was dying to loosen his collar. He felt as if he were choking. He must be sweating like a pig. It was ridiculous. He had had tons of interviews in the past. Aside from wanting to get a job, any job, he knew he was so agitated because he now really wanted this particular job. Having researched it, he'd discovered that, with his existing qualifications, all he needed to do to become a fully qualified librarian was complete a postgraduate librarianship course.

'So, do you have any other questions?' Patricia asked him. He'd already asked quite a few during the course of the interview, but now it appeared they were wrapping things up.

Evan looked at Patricia, then at Peter Finch, the IT Director for Newcastle City Council. 'Just one more. I'm keen to become a qualified librarian. I hear it's possible to get funding to do the librarianship postgrad course part-time whilst working. Is that something you're in a position to offer with this post?'

Weighing her words carefully, Patricia said, 'For the right candidate, yes, it would be possible.'

Heartened at Patricia's disclosure, Evan thanked her and Peter for their time and asked when candidates were likely to know if they had been successful.

'I'll email everyone, not only the successful candidate, by Christmas.'

'Great. Look forward to hearing from you.' Evan shook hands with them, before turning and leaving. He hoped he'd done enough.

'What did you think of her, Vic?' Daniel asked, once Star and Arianna had gone.

'She seems a nice girl. Do you think she'll be able to handle our little darlings?'

'I do, or I wouldn't let her look after them. Plus, I trust Star's judgement. It was nice of her to offer to bring Arianna here. I can understand why her mother wanted her to meet us first with an adult present. You can't be too careful.'

'No. Pity her mum has to work so much. She was a bit tight-lipped about her dad. Didn't you notice?'

'Maybe he's not around.' The irony of Victoria's comment regarding a parent working so much wasn't lost on Daniel. 'Anyway, at least she'll be here tomorrow afternoon to look after the kids so we can go Christmas shopping. I'm looking forward to it now.' Leaning forward and rooting around on the coffee table, he said, 'Where did I put that list? I've already lost it twice today!'

'I think you're sitting on it.' Victoria indicated a piece of paper poking out from underneath Daniel's trousers.

'Ah-ha! So, where were we? Maya?'

They resumed their chat about presents for their youngest, happy in the knowledge that the children were playing upstairs and unlikely to overhear.

Patricia closed the door behind her, drained. Five interviews. And she needed to do some admin before she finished tonight. Thank God she was off for two weeks after tomorrow. The irony didn't escape her. Prior to finding out about Ian's duplicity, she'd booked time off at Christmas for the first time in years, and now here she was with no plans. She could have gone to her daughter's in Wales. Megan had been more supportive than she could ever have imagined, and Graeme had invited her to spend Christmas with him and his family in London. It was the least he could do, he said. It was normally them coming home. Now it was his turn to host. But she didn't want to put her children in a tricky position. What if their father wanted to see them too? She didn't want to see him. Not on Christmas Day. The invitation to London had been tempting. She could have taken in a show, dined at some of the restaurants, enjoying cuisines she didn't find in Butterburn or Hawksmeade. Likewise, the thought of the Welsh capital had its pull. Yet she had remained undecided thus far.

As she waited for the kettle in the staffroom to boil, she spooned coffee into her bone china mug and sat down to leaf through one of the many magazines the library routinely received. As she drank her coffee, an advert for a writers' retreat caught her attention.

New Year's Resolutions – Writing Retreat – Lisbon 24 December to 3 January. All-inclusive. One-on-one tuition and feedback from qualified professionals and bestselling authors. No more procrastination, give it a go today!

A writing retreat. She'd always wanted to write. The most she'd ever submitted was a letter to the *Guardian*. But she knew if she were in the right environment, with like-minded people, she would be more inclined to write. Somehow she always found an excuse not to. Christmas Eve. Today was the twenty-first. Deciding for once to be impulsive, Patricia dialled the number on the advert.

CHAPTER SIXTEEN

'You've done what? What did you go and do that for? You know you're welcome here,' Megan said to Patricia.

'I saw the advert for it last night, called them up and booked it.'

'But then we won't see you over the holidays. The kids will really miss you being here.'

Patricia, feeling brave, said, 'Megan, you've been very good about this whole thing with your father, and I appreciate the support you've given me. I'd like for that to continue. This is something just for me. It feels right, and it's come at a time when things are pretty terrible for me. Could you please be happy for me? I've always wanted to do this.'

Megan listened to her mother's explanation, then after a long pause said, 'You're right. I…we'll just be so disappointed not to see you, that's all.'

'I know, and me you,' said Patricia, 'but I'll be back on the fourth and can drive down after that, or you can come here.'

'OK. Listen, Mum, have a good time. I mean it. You deserve it.'

'Thanks, darling. That means a lot to me. I'll text you when I arrive at the retreat, let you know I got there OK.'

Patricia said goodbye and held the phone in her hand for a few more moments, before finally replacing it in its cradle. This is the right thing to do, she thought. I need this.

'You be good for Arianna,' Daniel said, kissing Maya, then her two brothers in turn. Victoria followed suit, then Daniel helped her on with her sheepskin coat and they left. The delights of Christmas shopping three days before Christmas awaited.

'I want to play hide and seek,' said Maya.

'I want to play the Wii,' Dexter said.

'Well, I'm going to play with my Nerf gun,' said Riley, and left his two siblings in the living room with Arianna, as he went to fetch it.

When he returned, Arianna said, 'I think playing together might be fun. Why don't we play all of your games, starting with Maya's, as she's the youngest?'

The children surprised Arianna by agreeing and soon everyone was trying to hide in wardrobes, under beds and behind the coat stand.

Daniel and Victoria walked through the shopping mall in Hawksmeade, oblivious to the hordes of shoppers all around them. Daniel was determined they should enjoy the experience. It was the first time Victoria had been out of the house in months. He knew she'd have to take it easy and rest often, but he wanted her to participate and actively choose the children's toys with him. This past week or so she seemed to be doing so much better. There was a long way to go, and hopefully the psychologist in January would be able to help her progress further, but for now Daniel was revelling in the fact he and Victoria were behaving like ordinary parents.

He stopped outside Toy Emporium and gazed inside. There, taking centre stage, but with a hefty price tag, was the most fabulous rocking horse. Maya would love it. She loved anything to do with animals. He turned to Victoria, then pointed at the rocking horse. Victoria nodded. First decision made. Taking her hand, he entered the large toy shop, and they started browsing the aisles, looking for the perfect presents for their brood.

Patricia's mobile rang as she was preparing to go home and change for the party. Distracted, she picked up without checking to see who the caller was.

'I hear you're going abroad for Christmas.' Ian.

'That's right.'

'I hope you're not using our money to go.'

'That's a bit rich coming from the man who practically emptied our account.'

Clearly flummoxed, Ian stumbled over his words. 'I-I'm just saying. I was concerned about the kids. Graeme was very upset when he heard. You haven't even told him yet.'

Patricia hesitated for a fraction of a second. It was true, she hadn't had a chance to tell him. 'Ian, if you were so concerned about our children, you wouldn't have had an affair in the first place.' Her heart pounded. She felt sure he must be able to hear it. 'My plans are my plans. I haven't asked about yours.'

'I'm going to Graeme's.'

'I didn't ask.'

'I know.'

Patricia wondered if Karen was going too, or if she had her own family to visit. She tried to push the thought out of her mind. 'Look, Ian, I've got to go. It's the Christmas event tonight and I have to get ready.' And without waiting for a response, she hung up. There, she felt loads better already. As she left, she passed Star, who was one of the staff staying behind to ensure everything was ready for the party.

'I won't be long. I'll be back in plenty of time so you can change.'

'Take your time. I'll manage,' Star reassured her.

Once Patricia had gone, Star ensured there was adequate cover on the Enquiries desk, then went through to Scrolls to check the catering was under control. The van had arrived earlier from the suppliers, and all the platters had been loaded into Scrolls' fridges and freezers and onto work surfaces in preparation for the evening.

To celebrate the last in the library's Christmas themed days, there was the prerequisite mulled wine, as well as Christmas drinks from around the globe: creamy egg nog as favoured by the North Americans, glögg from Finland, Jamaican Sorrel punch, even some poppyseed 'milk' from Lithuania.

Returning to the main library, Star dimmed the stark overhead fluorescent lights and switched on the dozens of strands of blue and white Christmas lights she'd hung over the past few days. The tree looked magnificent now it was bedecked with many of the special decorations created by the children of the community, which they had hung on it after their masterclass.

Jessica came over. 'Star, this place looks amazing. Very atmospheric. How did you do it?'

Star gave a knowing little smile. 'I just love Christmas. That dress looks lovely on you. What an incredible shade of blue.'

'Thank you, Star. What a nice thing to say. Why don't you go and change? I can hold the fort here.'

'Thanks, I'll do that.' Star knew it wouldn't take long.

She dressed so quickly it was as if she had waved a magic wand, which wasn't far from the truth. Grey silk shift dress donned, she twisted her hair into an elegant chignon, spritzed herself with some floral eau de toilette, slipped on a pair of heels and went back into the library.

'So they behaved themselves for you?' Daniel asked.

'They were great. We had a ball, didn't we, kids?' said Arianna.

'Yes,' chorused the three children.

Victoria shared a complicit smile with Daniel, then Daniel turned his attention to Arianna. 'Could I have a word, please?'

Unsure if she had done something wrong, Arianna followed him into the kitchen.

Turning round to face her, Daniel said, 'You couldn't help me hide the presents somewhere, could you?'

Grinning, Arianna said, 'No problem. Where did you have in mind?'

. . .

Arianna arrived a little out of breath. It wasn't like her to take ages deciding what to wear, but this was a special occasion, so eventually she'd gone with skinny jeans and a red strappy top. She'd swapped her Converse for black ballet pumps she'd picked up at the discount supermarket with some of the money she'd earned babysitting for Daniel. It had been a lovely feeling being able to buy something new, and she'd enjoyed having her own money for a change. Maybe if the babysitting became a regular gig she would have enough money to go back to badminton club.

This morning she'd washed and blow-dried her hair, and her luxuriant black curls, which reached halfway down her back, still shone.

There were already quite a few people in the library, some she recognised, others she had never seen before, but no sign of Josh. Then she saw him. The faded blue jeans sat well on him, and the crisp white shirt made him look as if he'd stepped out of an advert for Persil.

'Hi,' she said, when she drew level with him. He smelled divine.

'There you are. You look beautiful.'

'Thanks. You don't scrub up too badly yourself.'

Mutual compliments over, Josh said, 'Hungry? The food looks good, very posh.'

Just then Arianna's stomach rumbled, betraying her. 'Er, yes, I'm starving. Haven't had a chance to eat yet.'

'How did the babysitting go?'

As they filled their plates with party food and Josh passed her a non-alcoholic fruit punch, Arianna told him about her day.

'How about you? What have you been up to?'

'Christmas shopping.'

'Ah, you're one of those, are you, leaving things to the last minute?'

'Not really, but I had a few presents still to get.'

'Oh, there's Star,' said Arianna. 'Star, beautiful dress. You look gorgeous.'

'Thanks, Arianna. I love your top. Very festive. Nice shirt, Josh. Very dapper!'

Josh reddened at the compliment and mumbled a thanks.

'The library looks fantastic. The strings of lights make it seem almost otherworldly. Did you do this?' Arianna asked.

'I helped,' Star said modestly.

'It looks like the ceiling is shimmering. Doesn't it, Josh?'

'Yeah, I'm not sure what you did, but it looks great.'

'Well, thanks, both of you. Have you had a look at the round-the-world collages?' Star pointed to the exhibits dotted around the library.

'I saw a few of them on their individual days, but I haven't seen them all together yet. I think we'll go and have a look now. See you later,' Arianna said. Josh followed her.

'These are pretty cool. Who did these, d'you think, the kids or the teachers?' Josh asked.

Arianna hid a smile. One of the things she loved about Josh was he found cool what many wouldn't, and certainly what many guys wouldn't admit to liking even if they did. Nor could she imagine many teenage boys going to a library Christmas party, but here Josh was, looking just as interested in the Christmas traditions of Scandinavia as her. She hadn't known Santa Claus was called *Julenissen* in Norway. She wondered if that was where the word 'yule' came from, if there was some connection. She'd google it later. And little gnomes called *Nisse* brought the presents. She liked the idea of that. Gnomes had bad press normally.

'A bit of both.' Arianna had seen some of the boards, as she'd spent so much time here, studying, and had perused many of them on the day they were erected. With the lights, the decorations, the tree which shone from its place in the middle of the room, and now reading about Christmas traditions around the world, it was hard not to feel Christmassy. Arianna bit into a cinnamon biscuit and proclaimed it so moreish, she dragged Josh with her to get another.

'Look at this one. In Egypt, Christmas is celebrated on 6 January, the same as in Russia. I didn't realise Egyptians celebrated Christmas.'

Arianna shrugged. She hadn't known either.

'And they have forty-three days of fasting when they don't eat any meat products! I could never be Egyptian. I'd starve. There's no chance of me ever being vegetarian.'

'What about this one?' Arianna pointed to the board two down from the Egyptian one. 'In Costa Rica, people decorate their houses with tropical flowers over Christmas and put a replica of the nativity in the middle. It's called a *Portal*.'

'Isn't it funny how the traditions are so different? Makes you wonder how they all came about.'

Arianna nodded her agreement and, cupping their hands around the warm fruit punch, which zinged in the mouth, they moved on to the next board.

. . .

Patricia, who had been caught up talking to various people since she'd returned from getting changed, finally managed to speak to Star.

'It's going rather well, isn't it? It's usually busy, but this year it's packed. I'm so glad you convinced me to order more food.'

'Yes, ever since we opened the doors it's been manic. Everyone seems to be enjoying themselves. There's been a lot of interest in the Christmas tradition exhibits, not only the alcoholic Christmas drinks.'

'Well, that's good, as no doubt we'll run out of alcohol first.'

'So, looking forward to tomorrow?'

'Yes, I can't wait.' Patricia had told Star first thing this morning, even before calling Megan. She had been desperate to share her good news with someone.

'What time's your flight?'

'Ten thirty, so not too bad. I won't be drinking more than two glasses of that lovely mulled wine, anyway, and I'm taking a taxi to the airport.'

'Wise move. So, do you need to take anything specific? Writing you're working on, that sort of thing?'

'No, just myself. They'll give us exercises there, show us how to make ourselves more receptive to writing. I bought a writing magazine on the way in this morning, so I can read that on the plane, get myself into the right frame of mind.'

Star looked at her friend. She was glowing. She was happy. Thoughts of her husband and his infidelity were, for now, forgotten. How true it was that when one door closed another opened. Without her separation from Ian, Patricia would never have taken this opportunity.

'Hi, Star, Patricia, I hope I'm not interrupting?'

'No, not at all, Evan. Good to see you here,' Patricia said.

Looking a little nervous, Evan thanked her and said how incredible the displays were.

'I couldn't agree more. Everyone involved has done a wonderful job, although much of the credit for the arrangements has to go to Star. She's worked closely with the schools on the project since she got here.'

'Well, she's certainly injected Christmas spirit into Butterburn.'

'Indeed she has. Well, if you'll excuse me, Evan, I can see a friend waving at me. I'll leave you with Star. Have a lovely Christmas.'

'You too.'

'Oh, and you might want to check your email.'

'Hi. I didn't realise you were coming to the Christmas event.'

'Didn't I mention it the other night?'

'No, you didn't.' Patricia smiled at Leo. 'So, have you sampled the Jamaican fruit punch?'

'Not had a chance yet. Why don't we get some?'

'Great idea.' And Patricia led Leo over to Scrolls.

'I've really enjoyed tonight,' said Josh, turning to face Arianna at the end of her street. 'I had no idea there were so many different Christmas traditions.'

'Me neither. And the food was good too.'

Josh grinned. 'Well, there is that. But that wasn't the best part.'

'Oh, no?' Arianna waited for him to elaborate.

'This is.' And Josh bent his head to Arianna's and kissed her, and kissed her, and kissed her some more.

Wow, thought Arianna. Wow.

CHAPTER SEVENTEEN

'Flight BA 502 to Lisbon now boarding from gate number twelve. Could all passengers please proceed to the boarding gate?'

Tucking her writing magazine into the front compartment, Patricia picked up her carry-on and made her way to the gate. Maybe this would be a new start for her. An adventure. A hobby of hers that could grow into something more. It would certainly be a different kind of Christmas, but this year that's what had been called for. She wouldn't miss the snow and the traditions. Thanks to Star she'd been surrounded by Christmas for the past month. If anything, she had Christmas overload, and she'd still get to do the present exchange with her children and have a meal when she got back. Plus they'd likely have a festive-themed meal on Christmas Day at the retreat. She'd printed off the literature the retreat organisers had sent her the day before and had been reading up on it at the airport. Twelve guests on this retreat. Not a huge number. Hopefully she would find someone to bond with so she didn't feel lonely. She'd felt brave when she booked it, but she was rather jittery now. Yet, at the same time, she couldn't deny an underlying excitement. She was going to write. She was going to spend time with fellow writers, exploring ideas and concepts. It would be heaven.

'Arianna. You in?' her mum called, when she returned from her night shift at the taxi office.

'Yep.' Arianna appeared, her curls still wet from the shower.

'How are you? Sleep well?'

'Not bad.' Although in truth Arianna had slept fitfully, her thoughts filled with Josh and that kiss.

'How was the party?'

'Well, it wasn't a "party" party, but it was really good. It was interesting to see how people around the world celebrate Christmas.'

'Was Josh there?' Arianna had mentioned Josh in passing a few times.

'Yeah. He had a good time too.'

'Did he walk you home?'

Her mum was fishing and they both knew it. Arianna nodded. 'He wanted to make sure I got in OK.'

Smiling, her mum said, 'Ah, before I forget, I have good news. Great news, actually.'

'Oh yeah?'

'I'm not working Christmas.'

'You're not?'

'No. Eileen's been invited to the Lakes at the last minute, so she's swapped me her Christmas holiday for my New Year one.'

'That's brilliant, Mum.' Arianna threw her arms around her mum's neck.

'I know. So, how about we decorate the tree tomorrow? I called and ordered one from Sykes. It'll be here in the morning.'

'Can we get out all the stuff from when I was little?'

'Of course. Why don't you go up into the attic and bring it all down? Then you can sort through it and decide which decorations you fancy putting on the tree this year.'

'I'll do that. Oh, Mum, this is going to be the best Christmas.' She kissed her on the cheek and hurried off to the attic.

Evan was euphoric. This interview signified change and hope. Perhaps there would be a bright future for him after all. The night before, when Patricia had said he should check his email, he hadn't been able to resist enabling his wireless connection on his phone to do so straightaway.

We would like to offer you the position of Librarian/IT Manager at Butterburn Library… Subject to a trial period, there will be the possibility to combine the post with the postgraduate librarianship course at the University of Newcastle… The email finished with, *Please confirm your availability to start on 7 January.*

Evan had breathed deeply, then gone to find Patricia to thank her, then done the same with Star, whose influence he felt certain had had some bearing on Patricia's decision, although she said he deserved all the credit as he had come across very well at interview. Then he'd gone straight home and broken the good news to Louise, who had hugged him and hugged him and said hadn't she told him something good was just around the corner. He'd thanked God he had such an understanding and amazing wife. Even the children seemed pleased at the news, but whether that was because they hoped they might receive the presents they had originally asked for, was anyone's guess. In any case, Christmas in the Donnelly household was bound to be a much happier event now.

Patricia was a jumble of nerves. She'd arrived at the retreat a couple of hours earlier, and after having a welcome drink with the organiser, Samuel Newden, she'd gone to lie down before dinner, when she'd meet the rest of the group. She dressed carefully for dinner – conservative in black trousers and a cream silk blouse, minimal make-up and her hair styled, but not elaborately so. Deciding she could put it off no longer, she closed her bedroom door and descended the staircase to the main part of the converted farmhouse.

She needn't have worried. Everyone was lovely. Within half an hour she felt as if she'd known them for months. Was she the only one who was rather reserved? she wondered. Mimi, a jolly hockey sticks kind of woman from Tralee in Ireland was a riot and kept regaling them with tales of the school where she worked. Cedric, a retired major who had to be eighty-five if he was a day, kept telling them of his time in Egypt. Vari was an undergraduate at the University of Southampton. Her parents had bought her a place on the writing retreat for her eighteenth birthday, which had been at the beginning of December. As Patricia met each of her counterparts, she realised that she was really looking forward to Christmas this year. New experiences. New friends.

The library was only open for a couple more hours, as it always closed at midday on Christmas Eve. Few people had graced it with their presence this morning, so Star was somewhat surprised to see Evan come in.

'You are keen to get started, aren't you?' she joked.

'I had some bits and pieces to get in town, and I wanted to thank you properly.' He handed her the spangly red gift bag he was carrying.

'You didn't have to do that. Thank you.'

'It's just a little something.'

'Do you mind if I open it tomorrow? I'm one of those that doesn't believe in opening presents early.'

'Not at all. Well, if I don't see you before then, I'll see you on the seventh.'

'Oh, is that your start date?'

'Yes. Are you doing anything special for Christmas?'

'I'm spending it with old friends.'

'Sounds good. The best kind.'

'Yes, I think so. Well, I hope you and your family have a lovely Christmas.'

'Merry Christmas, Star.' Evan turned, and with a nod of recognition and a mumbled Merry Christmas to Bridget, he was gone.

Star smiled. Excellent. Another one sorted. Evan would think he'd simply been in the right place at the right time. Of course, she knew different.

CHAPTER EIGHTEEN

'Daddy, Santa's been,' shrieked an overexcited Maya, as she climbed up on his bed. Riley was already bouncing up and down on the gap between him and Victoria, and even Dexter had perched on the end of the bed.

'Really?' asked Daniel, feigning surprise. 'Are you sure?'

'Yes, Daddy, I am. I heard his reindeer on the roof.'

'And I checked and he's eaten the biscuits we left him,' said Riley.

Not to be beaten, Dexter, usually so solemn, grinned and said, 'I've been into the living room and there are loads of presents!'

Deciding now was not the time to reprimand his eldest for breaking rank and going downstairs to check on Santa's deliveries, Daniel hugged his children to him, then Victoria, and said, 'Well, let's go and see what he's brought.'

'Yay,' his brood shouted.

They scrambled off the bed and, after throwing on his dressing gown, Daniel followed, with Victoria not far behind.

'Look at all those presents!' Riley was almost hopping with excitement.

Daniel directed the children to which presents they should bring over from the tree. He left his and Victoria's presents until last. They had been up until one o'clock wrapping everything and positioning it just so. They'd chosen different types of wrapping paper and gift bags so they would know at a glance which present was which. There were also three bed sheets covering larger presents, and Daniel could tell the children were anxious to know what was under them, but it was Maya who caved first.

'Daddy, why are there sheets in the living room?'

'Ah, those are extra-special presents from Santa. We'll open those last.'

The children continued to open their other presents: board games, games for their Wii, a science kit for Dexter, a three-foot soft-bodied Olaf from *Frozen* for Maya, a talking dinosaur for Riley. Eventually each child had amassed so many presents they had almost run out of places to put them. At this point it occurred to Daniel that they had perhaps gone overboard with the presents, but he had subconsciously tried to compensate for the year having been so awful for them all. Finally Daniel declared they could take the sheets off the larger gifts from Santa. He stood each child in front of the relevant sheet and said, 'After three. One, two, three.' Maya squealed when she saw the brown rocking horse with the luxurious white mane and wooden rockers and handles. Dexter gazed in awe at his new games console and television, and Riley already had one leg flung over his new flame-red bike.

Daniel looked at Victoria and they both smiled. He took her hand in his as they watched their children enthusing over their presents.

'Can I go out on it now, Dad, can I, can I?' asked Riley.

'Not yet, little man. The ground's still covered in slush, and it's freezing cold outside. Plus you're still in your pyjamas and slippers.'

'No problem,' said Riley, running into the hall and donning his Fireman Sam wellingtons.

'That's not what I meant,' Daniel told him, grinning. 'Let's see what it's like when we get back from church.'

The children played with their gifts for a while, then Daniel said, 'Who's for breakfast?'

'Me, me, me!' shouted the children, not making any attempt to move towards the kitchen as they would normally do.

'How about waffles?' Daniel said. A rare treat.

'With maple syrup?' asked Dexter.

'Of course with maple syrup!' Daniel's tone suggested there was no other way.

'Hurrah!' said Riley.

Soon the children scoffed the waffles and went back to their toys. That was one advantage to getting up at six o'clock; they had plenty of time to play before going to the Christmas service. Daniel loaded the dishwasher then went through to the living room where Maya was already rocking on her new horse, her mother by her side to ensure she didn't fall. Even in a week, Daniel had noticed a remarkable difference in Victoria. She wasn't as pale, and she was responding to the children, and she was up and moving around, not welded to the sofa. Dexter was leafing through his *5001 Amazing Things* book which Daniel had thought he might find interesting. Truth was, he'd liked the look of it, and figured he could do with knowing who invented the steam train, how many moons Jupiter had, and who Joseph Lister was. Riley was playing Operation by himself. Daniel surveyed the scene, and realised that although they still had a lot to sort out, he had a great deal to be thankful for.

'Daddy, come and play with me,' said Riley.

Daniel sat down beside his middle child. Taking the Operation tongs from him, he tried to remove the spare ribs, only for the buzzer to announce his failure.

'Ha, ha, Daddy, I can do it better than you. Look!' said Riley good-naturedly.

Daniel smiled as Riley removed the Adam's apple without a single sound.

'Well done, little man.'

Riley nearly burst with pride.

'Daddy, Olaf wants some waffles.' Maya pointed the large snowman at him. 'Can you make him some, please?'

Getting to his feet, Daniel took her by the hand, saying, 'Of course, sweetheart.'

'You look beautiful,' Daniel told Victoria, as he fastened her pearl necklace, stopping only to plant a swift kiss on her collarbone. Through the dressing table mirror in front of her, Victoria saw Daniel smiling at her, and she gripped his hand.

Things almost seem normal, Daniel thought. She looks more like herself, she's acting more like herself, please may it continue.

Victoria even helped Daniel dress the children in their Christmas finery: a green velvet dress for Maya, matching navy chinos and crisp, impractical white dress shirts for the two boys. The family went to church later that morning and Daniel found himself singing with gusto to both the hymns and the carols at the carol service which took place after Mass.

The sun had broken through the clouds whilst Daniel and his family had been at prayer, and it had turned into a beautiful, fresh December morning. The unexpected, but welcome sunshine had almost entirely obliterated the slush, so Daniel made an impromptu decision that they should all go for a walk before Christmas lunch. He knew it was more traditional to go for a walk after lunch, but he had a sneaking suspicion his little ones would be fast asleep by then.

He drove to the links at Hawskmeade and they walked along the promenade which bordered the golf course. Maya skipped along, an absolute angel, with her chestnut ringlets, which her mother had put in for her on Christmas Eve, her snow-white jacket in sharp contrast to the green velvet of her dress which poked out from underneath. Dexter and Riley were adorable – dressed in the same clothes, but barely looking like siblings at all. Riley's hair reflected his personality – it was all over the place. Daniel surveyed him and thought he might well be a boffin or nutty professor when he grew up. And Dexter, the quiet one, aside from his recent streak of violence at school, nipped in the bud after a quiet word from Daniel, just looked pensive. Daniel wished he knew what was going on inside his head, but lacking psychic powers, he did the next best thing. In two strides he came abreast of him and put his arm around his shoulders. Dexter didn't shrug it off, which Daniel took as a good sign. They walked for a mile or so, then Riley said that really if it was good enough weather to be out walking, he must be able to take his bike out too.

'Roo, I promise you can take your bike out when we get

home, OK?' Daniel said, mussing his son's hair to squeals of '*Dad!*'

Daniel followed his children into the house. By the time he'd dropped his car key on the hall table, Riley was already struggling past him with his bike.

'I'll be there in a minute, Roo.'

He'd toyed with the idea of cooking Christmas lunch from scratch but decided he was asking too much of himself. He wanted to enjoy the day and spend time with the children, not while away most of it in the kitchen, as they played with their toys in the living room. But he wanted it to be special. It was important to him they only retained good memories of this Christmas. OK, he realised their material needs had been more than met with the presents they'd received, but he recalled how, when he was growing up, Christmas dinner was one of the main events of the day, and one which he remembered fondly.

He'd called only a few days earlier, not expecting to have any success, but Red Grape Catering hadn't baulked at the short notice, and had been happy to provide staff and food. He'd left a key under the hedgehog solar light in the front garden. Not the safest option, he knew, but effective.

When he opened the kitchen door, the smell of roast turkey made him salivate, and after divesting the other two children of their coats, he went through to greet the caterers and see how they were doing. Three members of staff were bustling around. Daniel barely recognised it as his kitchen. There was amazing-looking food atop every surface. It seemed a long time since his breakfast waffles. He confirmed it was fine to have the starter in twenty minutes and went to help Riley ride his new bike.

. . .

Daniel was stuffed. He couldn't eat another bite. He couldn't move. The children had fallen asleep one by one, as the heat from the roaring log fire in the formal lounge, which they used only on special occasions, made them drowsy. He was close to joining them, but first he wanted to relax a little with Victoria. Snuggling down in the sofa, with his arm around her, he watched his children sleep and sighed with relief that Christmas had gone well.

CHAPTER NINETEEN

'Arianna.' Her mum shook her gently. 'Merry Christmas.'

Her tousled black hair streaming over the covers as she popped her head out from beneath them, Arianna stifled a yawn and said, 'Merry Christmas, Mum.'

'Do you want a cup of tea?'

'Yes, please.' Arianna put a hand over her mouth as she yawned again. She was so tired, but then that's because she'd been awake half the night thinking about Josh. Moving herself into a sitting position, she hugged her mum, who had now perched on the end of her bed.

'Right, I'll put the kettle on,' her mum said, getting up off the bed in one fluid movement.

Taking a few minutes before throwing her legs over the side of the bed, Arianna was spurred into action when her mum shouted from halfway downstairs, 'There are some presents in your stocking at the bottom of the bed.'

It didn't matter if you were six or sixteen, thought Arianna, those words were guaranteed to inject excitement into you. Hopping out of bed, she reached her stocking, which was deliciously twee: a large snowman whose buttons, carrot nose, and eyes had tiny pockets for holding treats. Chocolate money was in most of them, but a new mascara replaced the toothbrush she had been receiving for years. In the main section of the stocking, several small gifts were wrapped in Santa and penguin gift paper. Arianna threw on a pair of jeans and a long-sleeved top, then grabbed her stocking and joined her mum in the kitchen.

'Oh, haven't you opened them yet?'

'No, I wanted to open them with you.' This response brought a smile to her mum's face.

'Go on then,' her mum said, as she placed a cup of steaming hot tea in front of her.

Arianna delved into the stocking and pulled out a long, thin, rectangular box. It was a silver Cross ballpoint pen.

'It's lovely.'

'Glad you like it. I thought you could be doing with a decent pen with all the studying you have to do.'

Arianna nodded her agreement. The next one was a small jewellery box. Inside nestled a silver necklace with a pendant in the shape of an ocean wave.

'I love it. Oh thanks, Mum!'

'You're welcome.'

A diary came next, then the final present was an iTunes voucher. Now she could download the new Snow Ponies album. She'd wanted to after the concert the other night, but it had been months since she'd had any money to buy new music.

'Can we go and see the tree now, please? I put your present under it last night.'

Her mum smiled at her. 'Lead the way.'

It never ceased to amaze Arianna how her mum could make so much out of so little. The living room was warm and inviting. The decorations they'd hung the day before provided happy but bittersweet memories, as they highlighted her parents were no longer together. Decorating the tree had been a family ritual ever since she could remember. It was still a family ritual, but now that family generally consisted of two, not three, and it was even more evident this year with her father's absence. The tree was magnificent. They'd been lucky – the Norwegian spruce had been sixty per cent off, since they'd waited until the last minute. The baubles and trinkets they'd put up glittered, and a sense of magic hung in the air. Retrieving the gift she had bought for her mum from under the tree, Arianna held it out to her. 'Hope you like it.'

A fitted black wool cardigan fell out of the gift bag which she'd recycled from last year.

'It's gorgeous. This is too much. How did you afford this?'

'Babysitting.' It had been nice to get her mum something special. It had been pricy, but Daniel had already said he wanted her to babysit the following week, so she'd depleted all of her funds to get it. Her mum deserved it. She had so little. She rarely spent a penny on herself, preferring to buy Arianna things with any spare money she did have. Oh, her father paid child maintenance, but that went on the basics, and he wasn't around enough to take her out or treat her much. Christmas was the one time he rectified that, but not this year.

'Right, open the rest of your presents.'

Looking under the tree, Arianna saw there were more than she had expected.

She opened the first one and saw it was an iPhone from

her father. She didn't want to act like a spoilt child, but she couldn't get excited about it. Not at the moment. He wasn't here to enjoy Christmas with her, her mum was. So she wanted to open and enthuse over presents her mum had bought her. She opened the next one. A pair of jeans – excellent. She had three pairs already but they were all getting a bit threadbare at the hems from constant wear, and from trailing in the dirt, snow, slush. Next present. A camera.

She took in the array of presents still under the tree and said, 'Why are there so many presents this year?' Secretly she wondered if Mum had bought her a few extra presents to make up for her father's absence.

A smile broke out across her mum's face. 'Open this present and I'll tell you.'

Arianna took the envelope from her mum, opened it and read, '*London Theatre Breaks Ltd. 5 star reviews. Acclaimed performances by Delilah Meadows and Carson Tenant in the West End's favourite musical,* Cats. *Accommodation at the Excelsior hotel for 2 nights from 27 December to 29 December. First class return train travel from Hawksmeade to London Euston included.*'

Arianna turned to her mum, her face incredulous. 'Mum, how can we afford this? It's the trip of a lifetime.'

Her mum beamed, her cheeks pink with evident excitement. 'Joyce bought me five lottery tickets for my Secret Santa present. I got five numbers and won £1400.'

'Aaaaarggghhh!' said Arianna. 'We're really going!! I can't believe it.'

'I thought you deserved a treat. It's been a long time since we were able to do anything like this.'

The time to think of how that money could have been spent more wisely was for another day. For the moment

Arianna was delighted and couldn't wait for their theatre break. She hugged her mum and when she let go she was startled to see they both had tears in their eyes. This was turning out to be the best Christmas ever…just about.

Arianna downloaded the Snow Ponies' new album and lay back on her bed, her earbuds in. She was going to London. She'd never been to London before. She'd never been south of Birmingham, and that had only been to visit an ageing aunt. Her mum had regaled her with how they would have afternoon tea at the Dorchester and go to a posh restaurant for dinner. She really was making this a trip to remember. Her mum was the best. Just then, Arianna's phone rang. Checking caller display, she saw it was Josh.

'Merry Christmas,' Josh said, sounding as upbeat as ever. His level of chirpiness didn't exceed Arianna's today, though. After she wished him a Merry Christmas, too, she filled him in on her upcoming trip. She barely had time to get ready for it. She'd have to pack tomorrow, but today was for relaxing and enjoying time with her mum.

'That sounds like fun. I'm not a big musicals fan, but my mum loves them. She saw *Cats* a few years ago and said it was brilliant. You'll have a great time. And think about the flashy restaurant you'll be going to, and first class on the train. You might even be allowed a glass of champagne!'

Arianna didn't drink but felt certain her mum would permit it on such a special occasion.

'The reason I was calling, apart from to wish you Merry Christmas, was to ask if I could come round for a bit later, maybe about seven?'

Arianna said she thought that would be fine, but she'd check with her mum first and text him.

'Can you pass me out the gravy boat, please?' Arianna's mum asked.

Arianna knelt down and foraged in the cupboard next to the oven. 'There you go!' She raised it above her head and in the general direction of her mum, whilst she tried to rearrange the cups she'd knocked over.

'Thanks. Nearly done. Hope you're hungry.'

'I'm always hungry for Christmas lunch. There's just something about it.'

'Well, you made short work of that lentil soup, even though that's not Christmassy.'

'I was pretty hungry. I only had toast for breakfast, remember.'

'True. Right, let's get this to the table,' her mum said, carrying the small turkey in its roasting dish, surrounded by the parsnips, carrots and roast potatoes, over to the kitchen table, where Arianna had set two places. Arianna thought back to their old house with its separate, official dining room, but personally she preferred the dining kitchen here. This way she could talk to her mum, whenever she was home and cooking, or doing housework. It was a bit cramped, but it served its purpose, and today with the smell of the succulent roast turkey in the air, there was nowhere she'd rather be. She moved the red, green and gold Christmas crackers to the side, to allow her mum room to dish up. It really did look good.

They took their time over the meal, steering clear, for the most part, of anything which would involve bringing up the topic of her father. They talked about what was on TV later, but mostly they spoke of their imminent trip to the capital. After her phone call with Josh this morning, and whilst her mum was in the shower, Arianna had done a little research online. Oxford Street was the place to go. And she'd always wanted to visit Covent Garden, and let's not forget Piccadilly Circus. She'd checked out the hotel too: an opulent edifice on Park Lane. She couldn't wait for their trip. And she wanted to ensure her mum bought herself some things as well, maybe from Liberty or one of the other shops she would never normally frequent.

The dessert was shop-bought, but delicious nonetheless. Strawberry and champagne cheesecake. How appropriate for today's news and occasion. As they nibbled on their dessert, Arianna and her mum discussed what clothes they would take to London with them.

'Do you have anything suitable for going to the theatre?' Arianna asked.

Her mum laughed and said, 'It's not all *Last Night of the Proms*, you know. There won't be people there in tuxedos and ball gowns.'

Thinking that was exactly how some of them might be dressed, having seen performances of *Swan Lake* on TV where many of the theatregoers wore dresses and suits, Arianna pressed, 'So what *will* you wear?'

They continued discussing what might be appropriate to wear from their current wardrobes, as well as what else they might get up to in London, until the meal had been declared finished and the dishes, after a small hiatus, had been washed and left to dry on the rack.

'What do you fancy watching?'

'How about *Toy Story*? I love that film.'

'Your wish is my command,' said her mum, aiming the remote control at the TV.

The phone rang. 'I'll get it,' Arianna said.

'Hello?'

'Arianna?'

'Hi, Dad.'

'Merry Christmas.'

Having decided earlier that day to thaw and forgive her self-absorbed father, Arianna said, 'Merry Christmas, Dad. Thanks for my iPhone.'

'You're welcome. Have you had a good day?'

'Yes, the best.' She almost stopped herself, not wanting her father to feel miffed she had had such a good time in his absence. She didn't tell him about her mum's win, though. That was for her mum to share, if she wanted to. As she told him about Christmas dinner, she could practically hear him licking his lips on the other end of the phone.

'How has your Christmas been so far? What time is it there?'

'It's quarter past two. We're going to have Christmas lunch soon, but there's no turkey, I'm afraid. I believe we're having red snapper, although baked ham with pineapple and cherries has also been mentioned.'

'How's the weather?'

'Nice. Seventy-eight degrees. Not too hot, but no snow, about the same as this time of year in Dubai. Did you get a white Christmas this year?'

'No, but we did have snow until the day before yesterday. So what have you been doing this morning?'

'I took a walk on the beach. Kind of weird being somewhere like this on Christmas Day, to be honest.' He paused then said, 'I miss you, Arianna. I'm sorry. I won't do this again, to either of us. I wish I was there with you.'

'I wish you were here too, Dad.'

'I love you. I'll try to come over at half-term, OK, or maybe you can come over to me. I'll book a flight for you. Would you like that?'

Thinking of how she'd miss her mum, Arianna said, 'Let's agree to meet in February, Dad, but can we talk about where later?'

Her father agreed to this, and Arianna said goodbye, then after glancing at her watch, she settled back to enjoy *Toy Story*. Josh would be here in less than two hours.

A knock at the door signalled Josh's arrival. Arianna hit record on the remote and went to answer the door.

'Merry Christmas. Come in.'

'Merry Christmas.'

Arianna led him into the kitchen. Her mum, for once practising restraint, had remained in the living room, and hadn't tried to peek out to see what Josh was like. Arianna was quite impressed. She'd introduce them later.

'Do you want something to drink?' she asked. 'Or a Celebration?' She held the giant tin of chocolates out to him.

'Just a soft drink, thanks.'

Arianna poured some sparkling grape juice into a glass, then placed it in front of him.

'I have something I wanted to give you.'

Thinking back to the kisses Josh had given her, Arianna blushed.

He handed her a small, square box.

'I'm sorry, I didn't think to get you anything,' she said.

'Don't worry. We didn't say we were going to do presents, but I saw this and thought you'd like it.'

She opened it. Inside lay a snowman charm. He

must've noticed she was wearing her charm bracelet the other night. How thoughtful.

'It's beautiful, thank you.' She flung her arms around him, then pressed her lips to his.

'That's my present,' said Josh, grinning.

Arianna hugged him again. *This really has been the perfect Christmas.*

CHAPTER TWENTY

'Merry Christmas.' Evan snuggled into Louise, then turned her towards him and kissed her full on the lips.

'Ooh, I like where this is going. Merry Christmas to you too.' Louise planted her own smacker right on his lips. 'We don't get enough time like this, just the two…'

Her sentence was interrupted by the whirlwind that was Georgia, storming into their room.

'Mummy, Daddy, it's Christmas! C'mon. We have to get up. There'll be presents!'

Smiling at their daughter's lack of subtlety, Evan edged an arm out from under the covers to envelop her in a hug and wish her Merry Christmas. 'Now, go and wish Mummy Merry Christmas, then we can go and see about these presents.'

Georgia's noisy awakening of her parents had also roused Ryan, who appeared without the excitement emblazoned across his sister's face.

'Morning. Merry Christmas,' he drawled, as if it killed him to say so.

Evan smiled inwardly. Hopefully he would see a smile

on Ryan's face within the next half hour. It was Christmas after all.

They had barely time to admire the tree before Georgia was ripping at gift wrap and unearthing some of the toys her parents had managed to pick up for her. At least she hadn't peeked into the garden to see if a Welsh pony was hidden there for her, and it seemed she had come to terms with the fact that this year, again, there would be no equine addition to their family.

Ryan unwrapped his presents, mainly clothes, albeit minor designer brands, which still cost more than Evan could afford. A mumbled thanks was offered in return. Georgia found a Minnie Mouse plush toy and squealed with pleasure. Really, his daughter was easy to please, thought Evan. She'd just lost a sense of perspective for a while, as they'd given her so much in the past.

'Press her tummy,' said Louise, glancing at Evan in anticipation.

Georgia obliged and Minnie said, 'Merry Christmas, Georgia.'

Thrilled, Georgia said, 'Mummy, Minnie knows my name!'

Louise nodded. 'I wonder what else she knows. Why don't you press her tummy again?'

Georgia did as instructed and Minnie said, 'Georgia, would you like to come and see me skate?'

Georgia, brow furrowed in concentration, as if she was trying to work out how Minnie could possibly be so articulate, said, 'Yes, please.'

Getting the hang of this now, she pressed the doll's tummy again and it said, 'Would you like to come tomorrow?'

Georgia shrieked, 'Yes. Yes, please!'

She pressed the toy again and Minnie said, 'Your mummy and daddy have the tickets. Hope you enjoy the show.'

Grinning like buffoons, it was all Louise and Evan could do not to burst out laughing at the incredulous look on Georgia's face. Technology was amazing. Once Evan had found out he'd landed the job, he'd rushed out to buy a few extra gifts for the children, given they originally weren't getting much, and Louise had spent part of the previous night recording the message.

Even Ryan grinned on his little sister's behalf. He could see how pleased she was with the tickets.

'Oh, Ryan, sorry, I...' Catching Louise's meaningful glare, Evan revised that to, '*Santa* forgot to put this under the tree.' He winked at his son, then inclined his head towards Georgia.

Understanding, Ryan said, 'Right,' and took the envelope from his father. Turning it over, as if the back might yield some clue, Ryan, clearly stumped, opened it, withdrew the tickets, his brow creasing in confusion, before his face broke into a huge grin. 'How did you...? Know. Get these?' He didn't seem quite able to express himself. 'These are...'

'Like gold dust? I know.' Evan grinned at him.

Hugging his dad, Ryan said, 'Thanks.' Then, devouring the details of the Game Zone Exhibition on 29 December at the exhibition centre in Newcastle, he withdrew to the couch.

Louise exchanged a smile with Evan, the biggest gift of all. They hadn't bought each other gifts this year. Instead they'd agreed what little they did have they would spend on the kids. However, Evan also had an envelope for her.

'Open it,' he urged, pushing it towards her, drinking in the startled look on her face.

Louise did as he suggested, and took out a single sheet of paper which read,

To my beautiful wife – Merry Christmas – may we have many more. This letter entitles you to being waited on hand and foot for three days of your choosing, as well as the promise of a posh meal when my first pay cheque (proper one!) arrives. Your loving husband, Evan x.

Louise turned to him with tears in her eyes and said, 'That's the best present ever.' Then she whispered in his ear, 'You're the only present I need.'

As Evan embraced his wife, he said, 'Likewise.'

'How many people are going to be there, Daddy?' Georgia wanted to know.

'As far as I know, the old lady, Muriel, who lives at number forty-seven, and Grandad's friend, Hugh, and your cousins and aunt. I think that's it.'

'I miss Grandad,' Georgia said, after a brief pause.

'I miss him, too,' said Evan, a lump forming in his throat at the thought of his father, who had died five years previously.

'I wonder if Belle brought any of her toys,' she said, as she absent-mindedly twiddled one of Minnie Mouse's ears. Since Minnie gave her the good news, she had refused to put her down, almost as if she were fearful she might disappear, taking her Disney on Ice tickets with her.

'She's bound to have,' her mother said.

'We're here.' Evan pulled to a stop and put on the handbrake. They tumbled out of the car, gathering up presents, and the tureen of soup which was their offering for Christmas dinner.

Evan rang the bell and soon heard his mother's voice telling ten-year-old Belle to answer the door.

'Merry Christmas, Uncle Evan,' said Belle, who wore an adorable red dress with a white collar.

'Merry Christmas, Belle.' Evan crossed the threshold, set down the presents and hugged his niece. She smelled of chocolate. He suspected she'd delved into her selection box already. He moved past her into the hall, allowing the rest of his family to greet Belle, then went in search of his mother, whom he fully expected to find in the kitchen. He was right.

'Hi, Mum. Merry Christmas.' He kissed her on the forehead. She was shrinking, he was sure of it, but she was so full of vitality it was difficult to see on a day-to-day basis that she was getting old. Today she looked wonderful, resplendent in black velvet trousers, a white frilly blouse and a green tartan waistcoat. His mother certainly had her own style. Even at seventy-five she was an unstoppable force, the quintessential matriarch. This Christmas, more than ever, he was so happy to see her. As she held him to her, he breathed in her scent. *Jasmine.* Not for her the old-lady aroma of lavender.

'Merry Christmas, darling,' she said, seeming to understand that today was particularly difficult for him. 'Congratulations on the job, and also on the bank granting you a reprieve on the mortgage. You must be relieved.'

Evan had just time to indicate with his eyebrows exactly how much of a weight off his mind that was, before they were noisily interrupted.

'Gran, Merry Christmas!' Georgia barrelled into the room with Belle, followed by a smiling Ryan: Gran's boy.

They had always shared a special relationship, even when Ryan had been at his most brattish. Evan's mother took no nonsense from her grandson and always managed to keep him in line.

'Evan! Merry Christmas.' His gregarious sister, Jocasta, barged into the room, then enveloped her brother in a bear hug. 'I thought I heard your dulcet tones. How the he– on earth are you?' she said, seeing Belle and her impressionable niece in front of her.

'Good, Jo. You heard about the new job?'

'I did! Congrats. You must be pleased.'

'You have no idea.'

'And Lou, how lovely to see you.'

'Thanks, Jocasta. You too.' Louise allowed herself to be ensconced in a similar hug to that afforded to Evan.

'Shall we go through to the dining room? Muriel and Hugh are already here. We're all starving and dying to try this home-made soup we've been told you were bringing.'

'Lou's responsible,' said Evan.

'He's getting that in early, in case it's dire,' Louise said, laughing.

'I am not!' Evan feigned outrage.

'I'll get the drinks,' said Jocasta. 'What would you all like?'

'Muriel, Hugh, nice to see you again. You remember my wife, Louise? And the kids, Ryan and Georgia?'

'Oh yes,' said Muriel. 'You're Dorothy Stevenson's carer, aren't you, dear?'

When Louise nodded, Muriel said, 'Speaks ever so well of you. An angel, she called you.'

'I'll away and polish my halo,' joked Louise.

'No, but, kidding aside, she rates you very highly. You've got a good one there, Evan.' Whilst Louise blushed to the roots of her hair, Evan said with pride, 'I know,' and looked at her with tenderness.

'Gran, can we open our presents now?' Georgia, ever so subtle, asked.

'Of course, darling,' her grandmother said. 'Let me show you where yours is.'

'I can find it,' Georgia said, jumping up and running towards the lounge where the eight-foot tree dominated nearly a quarter of the room.

'I know you can, but I'd like to give it to you myself.'

Slowing to a brisk walk, Georgia waited whilst her grandmother walked in front of her, then bent down under the tree and withdrew a present which, at first glance, looked like a book. Georgia unwrapped it, her excitement fading. 'A book about horses.'

'Not just a book. Why don't you open it?'

Doing as her grandmother advised, Georgia turned the page and read, *For my beautiful granddaughter, a famous horsewoman in the making. Lots of love, Gran.*

She beamed at her grandmother, who said, 'Keep going.'

Georgia turned to the next page and found a leaflet, *Little Tipton Equestrian Centre – horse riding lessons for ages 4+.*

Georgia stared up at her grandmother, holding her breath, then it whooshed out of her, 'You mean…?'

'Every Saturday at half past nine. I'll take you. An hour and a half lesson.'

'I love you, Gran!' Georgia threw herself at her grandmother.

'I should hope so, and not only because I got you horse riding lessons for Christmas.'

'Oh no, Gran, I love you, anyway. I've always loved you.' The serious expression on her face made the others laugh.

'I'm glad to hear it. Now, if you'll let go for a second, I have something to give to your brother.'

With the smile never leaving her face, Georgia withdrew the terrier-like grip she'd had of her grandmother's leg.

'Ryan, I don't imagine you'll react in the same way as Georgia, but I think you'll be pleased.'

'Thanks, Gran,' mumbled Ryan. He wasn't one to show a great deal of emotion, unlike his exuberant sister. He took the envelope his grandmother handed to him and opened it. Out fell five crisp ten-pound notes.

'Cheers, Gran.'

'You're welcome, darling,' she said, as he kissed her wrinkled cheek. 'But that's not all that's in there. Look again.'

Puzzled, Ryan put his hand inside the envelope and withdrew a single sheet of paper. In it was a contract.

Goal: to own a PlayStation 4

I, Paula Donnelly, will contract my grandson, Ryan Donnelly, for gardening and other chores at a rate of £5 per hour, as and when required.

Ryan looked at his grandmother. He knew she was quirky and had a great sense of humour. She'd just given him fifty quid as his Christmas present. Doing the calculations in his head, he could own a PlayStation 4 by working less than fifty hours.

'Thanks, Gran. I take it loading the dishwasher today doesn't count?' A look from his grandmother had him saying, 'Well, you've got to try, haven't you?'

'You're right,' his grandmother said, stroking his hair, 'it doesn't. But don't worry, I intend to clear out the attic in the New Year. That should give you a few hours' work.'

Ryan thanked his grandmother again, then went to fetch drinks for the children, delighted with the notion that relatively soon he would be the owner of a PlayStation 4.

'That was a nice thing you did, Mum,' Evan said to her, when he caught up with her in the kitchen later. 'Actually, two nice things.'

'Only two nice things?' she teased.

'You know what I mean. Thanks. For everything.' And Evan laid his head on his mum's shoulder and sobbed, great wracking sobs, letting out all the tension of not only the past couple of months, but the past couple of years. He was thankful for his mum's support, and so touched she had gone out of her way to provide the children with what he couldn't – not this year – but without being over the top about it, or giving them everything, so they wouldn't be spoilt brats. Georgia may have to keep dreaming about her pony, but dream she could, now she had the horse riding lessons. His mother had also enabled Ryan, putting his desire to own the latest games console within his reach, but without handing it to him on a plate – genius. And it didn't make Evan feel such a failure, which he guessed had also been one of the reasons she had done it in the way she had. She was one in a million. He stared into her eyes, trying to will the words to come, but he didn't know how to start, so he said simply, 'I love you, Mum.'

'I know, son. I love you too.'

And they held each other for a few moments more, each glad to be with the other on this special day.

The assembled company pulled crackers, read out jokes, and Ryan put himself in charge of music, whilst Belle professed herself queen of the TV remote. The adults remained around the dining table long after the meal was over. Jocasta kept the drinks topped up. The children played together, with no bickering. Hugh brought them up to date with the local gossip: who had asked for planning permission to add on a garden room, who was off to the Azores on holiday for their sixtieth birthday, who was likely to win the darts tournament at the Whistlestop pub. Evan surveyed the scene, took Louise's hand in his and pressed it to his lips, feeling truly grateful that these were his family and friends.

CHAPTER TWENTY-ONE

'Now since you all know each other, I won't bother going through everyone's names again. Yes, I saw you all in the bar until late,' joked Samuel. 'In any case, there are name cards on the tables for those of you who over-imbibed last night and can barely remember your own name, let alone anyone else's!' This earned some laughs from the assembled group. 'So why don't we start with an exercise which is very topical? Describe in five hundred words or less your ideal Christmas Day. I want you to think about sights, sounds, smells, emotions, as well as presents. What can you visualise? And just as importantly, what helps your readers do so?'

Until she was on the plane with her writing magazine, Patricia hadn't written in years. The magazine contained a few exercises and writing suggestions which she had tried en route to Portugal. Now she conjured up the smell of pine needles: Christmas meant a real tree. The aroma of mulled wine, cinnamon, cloves. The feeling of goodwill that seemed to last from a couple of days before Christmas until shoppers would cut you dead at the Boxing Day sales. A white Christmas. The love she had for her children and how she always felt lucky they chose to spend the holiday with her and their father. She hoped she wasn't letting them down this year. But no, they'd been surprised, but in the end supportive. They wanted her to do what was best for her.

'OK, I realise this is all very personal–' said Samuel, after twenty minutes had elapsed and he had checked they had all finished their piece '–but is anyone happy to share even one item from their list?'

Mimi was first up. 'I think of drinking malt whisky instead of sherry, and the sing-song we have, if one whisky turns into five.'

'Good, Mimi, thank you. Anyone else?'

'I think of dipping marshmallows in Spanish hot chocolate,' said Vari, 'and of how when I was a young child, I used my father's hat, scarf and gloves for my snowman, and how he went to my gran's on Christmas Day in his second-best set as he didn't want to upset me by taking them off.'

Chuckles were heard around the room at this, and a loud, 'Aw, that's so cute!' from Mimi.

Patricia thought so too. 'I think of how much I love my family and how blessed I am that we're all together,' she said. A few eyebrows knitted together at this and she realised their confusion. 'This year's a bit of a one-off.'

'Hell, we've all had those.' Mimi nodded sagely.

Embarrassed for having spoken about her emotions so openly, and wondering where it had come from, Patricia bowed her head and pretended to study what she had written.

.   .   .

'It's quite enlightening, isn't it?' said Mimi to Patricia at lunch, as she twisted spaghetti vongole around her spoon.

Patricia nodded. 'It's surprising how much you can write when you're forced to do so.'

'I know, and it's cathartic too. Sorry, I didn't mean to sound poncy. I'm not in therapy or anything crazy like that. Hate all that American claptrap. Wait a minute! You're not in therapy, are you?'

'No.' Patricia smiled at her.

'Thank God for that. I thought I'd put my size sixes in it.'

'You haven't.'

'Quite the mixed group we've got here, isn't it?'

Patricia agreed it was. There was only one person she wasn't overly keen on and it was a woman who came across as boastful and very confident. If she were stereotyping she'd say she didn't look like someone who would spend Christmas at a writers' event. In fact she wouldn't think her a writer at all, but she supposed it took all sorts. She had the air of someone who would be more at home skiing in Lake Tahoe or holidaying in Mustique.

'So, do you wonder what their stories are?' Mimi asked.

Patricia looked at her. What was Mimi's story? She came across as both brash and bubbly at the same time, but Patricia reckoned there might be a vulnerable side to Mimi. Wasn't there always with people who were so extroverted?

'Of course. But they'll tell us about themselves if they want to.'

'Wise words,' Mimi said, 'but doesn't the writer in you make you want to invent their story, until you know what it is?'

Patricia considered this. 'I suppose it does. Don't we all

make assessments of people when we meet them? Judgements?'

'I'd say we do.'

Their conversation was halted by Thierry, the only Frenchman in the group, asking in his unaccented English if he could join them. Her chat with Mimi had made Patricia realise something. What if she wasn't as blameless in the breakdown of her marriage as she thought? She hadn't been unfaithful, but had she perhaps not listened when Ian was talking to her? Had they grown apart without her noticing? She needed to reflect upon this. Had there been cues she hadn't picked up on? Should she judge Ian less harshly, and simply let him get on with his life, in a way forgiving him? She'd undoubtedly feel better for it, and could let go of the resentment she felt, a poison which ate at her very soul.

Brought back to the present by Thierry asking her if she would like a drink, Patricia thought maybe she could forgive, but she knew she would never forget.

'So, have any of you heard of the Pomodoro technique?' Samuel asked, once they had taken their places again.

A few hands shot up. Samuel asked Vari to explain the merits of it to the others.

'Well, it's so we don't procrastinate. It breaks everything down into twenty-five-minute chunks, which makes them more manageable, and when we achieve our goals, it makes us feel better.'

'Excellent, Vari. That's pretty much it in a nutshell.' Samuel then went on to discuss how it might work for some, but not everyone. For instance, a writer with very young children might not manage to write for twenty-five minutes at a time, and might instead have to be satisfied with grabbing ten minutes whenever they could. Many around the table nodded, particularly those who were parents.

'So, here's a task for you. Think of your favourite book. Done? How could you turn it into a screenplay? Let's jot down some thoughts on how to convert from one format to another, and we'll discuss in a couple of minutes.'

Animated discussion instantly broke out.

'Oh, and obviously it has to be a book which hasn't already been made into a film.'

There were some groans at this, but then they all applied themselves to the task, with much chewing of pencils, tapping of pens, and looking at the ceiling, as well as some furious scribbling. Samuel had intimated at the beginning of the course that for the first part of the week they were going back to basics, no computers. It was odd, but liberating at the same time. Whilst it posed no problem for some in the class who had always written by hand, others were finding it hard going.

By the time classes finished for the day, Patricia was exhausted. She thought a nap before dinner would be a good idea, but Mimi was having none of it.

'C'mon. We can sleep any time. I know I'm bullying you, but hopefully in a good way,' she said, taking Patricia by the arm, and smiling at her. 'Those seats over there at the bar have our names written all over them.'

Dinner was at seven thirty. Cedric, Vari and a few of the others had joined Mimi and Patricia for a while, then they all went their separate ways to change for dinner. As part of their package, Samuel had arranged a special meal in a *taverna* close by. Thierry had been talking all afternoon about the famous salt cod served there. They were the only visitors that evening and the special Christmas Eve menu which the taverna had prepared for them was beyond expectation. Patricia initially hadn't enthused much at the prospect of salt cod, although she did like fish, but the *Bacalhau à Gomes de Sá*, a more palatable version than the traditional *Consoada*, for tourists, had proved delicious. With a plentiful supply of port, and a selection of Christmas cakes which had them all promising to join a gym in the New Year, they were well catered for.

Conversation flowed and Samuel explained how, if they wished, they could go to midnight Mass at the nearby *Igreja de Santa Maria* and witness the traditions there. The minibus would bring them back to the *pousada* later. Mimi was Catholic, so she said she would like to go, and Patricia decided she would tag along. As they all chatted about the various Portuguese Christmas traditions, Thierry and Chiara both jumped in with traditions in Italy and France, which the Brits weren't au fait with. Cedric was aghast at presents being put inside people's shoes, declaring it most unhygienic. Everyone laughed, and Chiara, who came from a little village ten kilometres outside Naples, told of how her father owned a company which made cribs and figurines for the nativity. Apparently Naples was the centre of the Italian crib-making world. Patricia listened to all of this with great interest.

'We eat our main meal, *Réveillon*, after midnight Mass,' said Thierry.

'Whereabouts in France are you from?' Patricia asked.

'I am from Brittany,' he said proudly. 'I am Breton. Usually we have roast turkey with chestnuts. It is delicious.' His English was excellent. 'But sometimes we have goose.'

'I've never had goose,' said Cedric. 'Noisy things.'

Patricia fought to suppress a laugh. Cedric's eccentric behaviour and demeanour suggested he should be wearing a three-piece suit and have a pocket watch which he kept in his waistcoat, but he was wearing jeans and a T-shirt which said, *I know more than you think and less than I'd like*. He was such a contradiction.

Patricia nibbled at a piece of *bolo rei*, king cake, and groaned. She had eaten too much already, but it was so good. She looked around the assembled company and knew she had made the right decision in spending Christmas here.

It was late when they left the taverna, so the minibus went straight to the church to drop off those who wished to attend the midnight service. There would be no classes on Christmas Day, as the main meal in Portugal was a Christmas lunch, which they would have at the retreat itself. Patricia didn't know if Samuel and his staff were cooking the meal or if they had hired caterers, but she was looking forward to it. She was making new friends here, having new experiences and learning a lot about herself.

In the end they all went to midnight Mass. As a group they were loath to break up and everyone agreed it would enrich their Portuguese experience. They tumbled into the pousada at quarter past two. Mimi tried to convince them all to have a nightcap, but this time Patricia and the others, worn out, would not be swayed. They bade each other goodnight and Merry Christmas and headed for bed.

Only when she'd reached her room did Patricia realise

she'd left her phone on the bedside table earlier. She had a text from Megan. *Merry Christmas, Mum. Hope you're having a great time. Call you later x*. Patricia smiled. Although she was having a lovely time, it was good to know Megan was thinking of her. She felt a pang of guilt at the fact she hadn't thought of her family since before she left for dinner. But surely that meant she was coping better? She was about to put on her nightdress, when she saw she had a voicemail too.

'Trish. It's me.' Ian. What was he doing calling her? 'There's no other way to say this. I've made a mistake. I love you.' Patricia listened to the rest of the short message, and sat back on her bed. Well, that was one way to burst her bubble. Glad she hadn't had so much to drink that she was tempted to ring him back, Patricia got into bed and struggled to fall asleep.

When Patricia woke next morning, she initially didn't remember where she was. Then it all came back to her, how it was Christmas morning, and how Ian had called her the night before. What was she meant to do with that declaration? Checking her watch, she saw it was quarter to ten, the latest she'd slept in a long time. Once she'd finally fallen asleep, she'd slept remarkably well, although she'd been dreaming of her early days with Ian, and all of a sudden he would morph into a current-day Leo. It was all very confusing. A shower would sort her out, she thought.

When she came out of the shower, there was a note lying just inside her door.

I didn't want to knock in case you were still sleeping (magnanimous of me, I know!). I'm in the café bar, if you're interested. Samuel has laid out a buffet-style breakfast for latecomers. Mimi.

Mimi was a tonic, even if a bit full-on. She did what others were too afraid to do, and oozed confidence. Patricia liked her a lot. She hoped they would remain friends after the retreat was over and felt glad it had only just begun.

'Merry Christmas, darling,' Patricia said, when Megan answered the phone.

'Merry Christmas, Mum. How are you doing?'

Patricia gave Megan a brief rundown of the events of the previous day and night.

'You went to Mass?'

'Yes, it was really nice. There were quite a few children there too, which I found strange, but apparently they get to open a couple of gifts when they get home from the service, and then the rest in the morning. So how's the clan?'

'Busy. Lisette's playing with her princess tablet and Xavier is building towers with blocks.'

'Ah, sounds quite sedate for your lot. Christmas dinner under control?'

'Yes. Just got to shove the turkey in the oven in about ten minutes, then start prepping the veg.'

'Well, listen, I'll let you go. I haven't even had breakfast yet.'

'Mother, you absolute stop-out!'

For some reason Patricia's thoughts turned to Leo. 'Not at all, just having a lie-in. Enjoy the rest of your Christmas, darling. Give my grandchildren a kiss from me, and a hug for Justin.'

'Will do, love you. Bye.'

· · ·

'So, what's eating you?' Mimi asked as they sat sipping espresso.

'Sorry?' Patricia asked.

'You were miles away.'

'Sorry.'

'No need to apologise. Can I help? Problem shared and all that.'

Sighing, Patricia said, 'How long have you got?'

'However long it takes.'

When Patricia got to the end of her story, Mimi said, 'Well, you are in a pickle. And nothing's happened between you and this Leo guy?'

Patricia shook her head.

'Here's what I think. You have another ten days on this retreat. I think you should enjoy yourself, give yourself time to think properly, whilst you're away from it all. I wouldn't call your husband back, not even to wish him Merry Christmas. Let him stew. If he's serious, and you decide you want him back, then he'll keep. You haven't done anything wrong, although I'm guessing you've already imagined Leo naked.'

'Mimi!' Patricia feigned outrage, because, of course, she was right. But unlike Ian she hadn't acted upon it, and it wouldn't have crossed her mind if she and Ian had still been together.

'A little distance will give you perspective and a clearer head to make decisions.'

Mulling this over, Patricia came to the conclusion it was pretty solid advice.

. . .

As Patricia tucked into her roast pork at lunch later that day, Mimi's words went round and round in her head. She didn't have to make up her mind right now. Could she live with Ian again after what he'd done? Would others think her a doormat? Would he do it again? And then there was Leo, or the promise of Leo. As she placed another forkful of the succulent meat in her mouth, she smiled as she thought of the dilemma she was in: take Ian back, or start something new. At the beginning of December she'd been a mess and dreading Christmas. Now, here was the day itself. She was happy, she was with new friends and she was in control of her own destiny. Whatever happened in her love life in the future, she would be the one making the decisions. Patricia raised her wine glass and toasted herself.

CHAPTER TWENTY-TWO

Star loved this time of year. Yet at the same time she felt sad, as her stay here was almost over. Having assured her charges' festive happiness, it was time for her to move on. She did, however, get to choose two things: a new name for next year and a holiday destination for January. Her work at Butterburn was done.

She'd used her magic snow globe to check up on everyone's Christmas Day and had been delighted to see that Daniel, Arianna, Evan and Patricia would be just fine.

She hadn't been lying to her colleagues that she was spending Christmas with old friends. Replete after her Christmas meal, Star topped up her sherry glass and decided to have a peek at last year's beneficiaries in Winstanton. Christmas Day was the only day she was able to do so, and she looked forward to it for months. She had to try to be as unobtrusive as possible. She didn't want them noticing her, although Jacob and Tabitha had seen her last year. She'd check on them last. She selected a red and gold bauble from the tree, held it in both hands and gazed upon the scene before her. Meredith. Ah, she was still with her family, excellent. But this time instead of being at her sister's house, workaholic Meredith was hosting the party. Some of the faces from last year were there, but there were new ones too. And Meredith looked quite at home in that apron. Who would have thought it? A year ago she'd have had the help do the cooking. It would never have occurred to her she could or should do it herself. She'd gained a little weight, too, and it suited her. Ah-ha, who was this? Star knew tall, dark and handsome was a clichéd description for a man, but this one was. When he bent his head to Meredith's and kissed her softly on the lips, Star smiled. She'd always known Meredith wasn't quite the ice maiden everyone made her out to be, and clearly she'd thawed.

Another bauble. Royal blue with white frosting. Another life. Stanley. Stanley seemed a little frailer. He was using his stick more. But he looked happy. He was sitting at his friend George's table spooning roast potatoes onto his plate. So his new friendship, born out of the club he had joined, had lasted. Star had a glimpse of him that morning, laying pink carnations at his beloved wife's grave. Christmas would always be tough for him, she knew. It was hard for all of those who had lost loved ones. Yet it was easier when surrounded by good friends. She watched as Stanley told George that his grandson was coming back to visit from Canada again at Easter. It was good to see his family were continuing to include him in their lives – despite the distance.

Next it was Rebecca's turn. A green on gold bauble. And there she was, thriving in her new position as Assistant Manager at The Melbourne Gallery, if her demeanour today was anything to go by. She'd sworn off men after her split from Ethan. But wait. Yes, the chap next to her in the pub had definitely touched her arm in a proprietorial fashion.

So, a new love interest for Rebecca too. The thought warmed Star's heart. Sometimes when you opted to shut yourself off from love, it came to you.

Taking one final bauble from her tree, and savouring it, there then appeared before her images of Jacob, Sophie, Tabitha and a baby, around six months old. Jacob was sitting on the arm of the sofa, whilst Sophie, who now sported an engagement ring, leant against him. Tabitha was wearing a smart, asymmetrical striped black and royal blue sheath dress, but she had a practical muslin cloth slung over one shoulder. The baby wore a beautiful pink dress and her chubby little thighs were encased in pink and white spotty tights. She was shaking a rattle and giggling. Star smiled. The rattle was the antique one she had given Tabitha before the baby was born. Star's time as Christmas Spirit was coming to an end. The rattle ensured the baby would always have Christmas spirit and imbued her with the powers she'd need in years to come. Baby Lara – the Christmas Spirit of the future.

Did you get your free short stories yet?

TWO UNPUBLISHED EXCLUSIVE SHORT STORIES.

Interacting with my readers is one of the most fun parts of being a writer. I'll be sending out a monthly newsletter with new release information, competitions, special offers and basically a bit about what I've been up to, writing and otherwise.

You can get the previously unseen short stories, *Mixed Messages* and *Time Is of the Essence*, FREE when you sign up to my mailing list at www.susanbuchananauthor.com

Did you enjoy *Return of the Christmas Spirit*?

I'd really appreciate if you could leave a review on Amazon or Goodreads. It doesn't need to be much, just a couple of lines. I love reading customer reviews. Seeing what readers think of my books spurs me on to write more. Sometimes I've even written more about characters or created a series because of reader comments. Plus, reviews are SO important to authors. They help raise the profile of the author and make it more likely that the book will be visible to more readers. Every author wants their book to be read by more people, and I am no exception!

ALSO BY SUSAN BUCHANAN

Have you read them all?

Sign of the Times

Sagittarius – Travel writer Holly heads to Tuscany to research her next book, but when she meets Dario, she knows she's in trouble. Can she resist temptation? And what do her mixed feelings mean for her future with her fiancé?

Gemini – Player Lucy likes to keep things interesting and has no qualms about being unfaithful to her long-term boyfriend. A cardiology conference to Switzerland changes Lucy, perhaps forever. Has she met her match, and is this feeling love?

Holly is the one who links the twelve signs. Are you ready to meet them all?

A tale of love, family, friendship and the lengths we go to in pursuit of our dreams.

The Dating Game

Work, work, work. That's all recruitment consultant Gill does. Her friends fix her up with numerous blind dates, none suitable, until one day Gill decides enough is enough.

Seeing an ad on a bus billboard for Happy Ever After dating agency 'for the busy professional', on impulse she signs up. Soon she has problems juggling her social life as well as her work diary.

Before long she's experiencing laughs, lust and … could it be love? But just when things are looking up for Gill, an unexpected reunion forces her to make an impossible choice.

Will she get her happy ever after, or is she destined to be married to her job forever?

The Christmas Spirit

Natalie Hope takes over the reins of the Sugar and Spice bakery and café with the intention of injecting some Christmas spirit. Something her regulars badly need.

Newly dumped Rebecca is stuck in a job with no prospects, has lost her home and is struggling to see a way forward.

Pensioner Stanley is dreading his first Christmas alone without his beloved wife, who passed away earlier this year. How will he ever feel whole again?

Graduate Jacob is still out of work despite making hundreds of applications. Will he be forced to go against his instincts and ask his unsympathetic parents for help?

Spiky workaholic Meredith hates the jollity of family gatherings and would rather stay home with a box set and a posh ready meal. Will she finally realise what's important in life?

Natalie sprinkles a little magic to try to spread some festive cheer and restore Christmas spirit, but will she succeed?

Just One Day – Winter

'Perfect for fans of *Why Mummy Drinks*.'

Thirty-eight-year-old Louisa has a loving husband, three wonderful kids, a faithful dog, a supportive family and a gorgeous house near Glasgow. What more could she want?

TIME.

Louisa would like, just once, to get to the end of her never-ending to-do list. With her husband Ronnie working offshore, she is demented trying to cope with everything on her own: the after-school clubs, the homework, the appointments … the constant disasters. And if he dismisses her workload one more time, she may well throttle him.

Juggling running her own wedding stationery business with family life is taking its toll, and the only reason Louisa is still sane is because of her best friends and her sisters.

Fed up with only talking to Ronnie about household bills and incompetent tradesmen, when a handsome stranger pays her some attention on her birthday weekend away, she is flattered, but will she give in to temptation? And will she ever get to the end of her to-do list?

A feel-good, heart-warming story of family and friendship. Ideal for fans of Fiona Gibson.

'This fresh, well-paced story will have you groaning in sympathy as things go from bad to worse.'

Book Escapes BabsW67

Printed in Great Britain
by Amazon

82080557R00116